SPECIAL MESSAGE TO READERS

This book is published under the auspices of

THE ULVERSCROFT FOUNDATION

(registered charity No. 264873 UK)

Established in 1972 to provide funds for research, diagnosis and treatment of eye diseases.

Examples of contributions made are: —

A Children's Assessment Unit at Moorfield's Hospital, London.

•

Twin operating theatres at the Western Ophthalmic Hospital, London.

•

A Chair of Ophthalmology at the Royal Australian College of Ophthalmologists.

•

The Ulverscroft Children's Eye Unit at the Great Ormond Street Hospital For Sick Children, London.

You can help further the work of the Foundation by making a donation or leaving a legacy. Every contribution, no matter how small, is received with gratitude. Please write for details to:

THE ULVERSCROFT FOUNDATION,
The Green, Bradgate Road, Anstey,
Leicester LE7 7FU, England.
Telephone: (0116) 236 4325

In Australia write to:

THE ULVERSCROFT FOUNDATION,
c/o The Royal Australian and New Zealand
College of Ophthalmologists,
94-98 Chalmers Street, Surry Hills,
N.S.W. 2010, Australia

TERROR TOWER

Worryingly for Scotland Yard, four officers disappear whilst on duty. One vanishes chasing a forger. Then two officers disappear searching for a wanted jewel thief in Hythe. Finally, a fourth officer vanishes in Hythe, after being sent to the nearby village of Stonehurst. Criminologist Trevor Lowe investigates a lead: someone has telephoned to arrange a meeting at the crossroads between the two villages. Lowe keeps the rendezvous but finds the man has been silenced — shot dead in a ditch . . .

Books by Gerald Verner
in the Linford Mystery Library:

THE LAST WARNING
DENE OF THE SECRET SERVICE
THE NURSERY RHYME MURDERS

GERALD VERNER

TERROR TOWER

Complete and Unabridged

LINFORD
Leicester

First published in Great Britain

First Linford Edition
published 2011

British Library CIP Data

Verner, Gerald.
Terror tower. - - (Linford mystery library)
1. Great Britain. Metropolitan Police Office.
Criminal Investigation Dept- -Fiction.
2. Criminologists- -England- -Fiction.
3. Police- -Violence against- -England- -
Fiction. 4. Detective and mystery stories.
5. Large type books.
I. Title II. Series
823.9′12–dc22

ISBN 978–1–4448–0695–3

Published by
F. A. Thorpe (Publishing)
Anstey, Leicestershire

Set by Words & Graphics Ltd.
Anstey, Leicestershire
Printed and bound in Great Britain by
T. J. International Ltd., Padstow, Cornwall

This book is printed on acid-free paper

1

Jim Winslow Comes to Stonehurst

A crowd of villagers congregated outside the Crossed Hands, the ancient timbered inn that stood in Stonehurst's narrow high street. Men with rugged faces and rough clothes, whose gnarled hands and broken nails testified to lives mostly spent in wresting a living tilling the soil. Apparently there was some kind of trouble afoot, for old John Tarley, waving the remains of a pint of beer in the air to add weight to his words, was telling the group around him exactly what he thought about it.

'Ain't none o' ye got no respect for the place where you was born and bred?' he cried in a deep voice that occasionally broke into a piping treble as he got more excited. 'What's goin' to 'appen if they're allowed to build a factory right in the heart of the village? I'm tellin' ye, life won't be worth livin', and that's drawin' it mild.'

''Course it will,' chimed a voice from the back of the group. 'Anyone with 'alf an ounce of sense can see that. A fine factory 'ull turn Stonehurst from a village to a prosperous town. I'm all for progress, I am.'

A murmur of voices went up, some in heated argument and others loudly bellowing applause. The camp was evidently a mixed one.

'You're wrong, and I'm tellin' ye,' roared John Tarley, raising his voice to make himself heard above the others. 'We'll 'ave the place full of them smoky chimneys, motor-vans and offices of works an' all. They ought to keep them sort of things up in the Midlands where folk 'as got factories, and such like things, in their blood. Mark my words, if they're allowed to build a factory 'ere, it'll be the farmers what'll pay for it. All o' you earn yer keep off the land, but there won't be no land worth a button when they start buildin' all round. The folks wot 'ave got their livelihood from the soil will find themselves elbowed off the map, and don't you make no mistake — ' He broke off, his face flushed with excitement, and moistened his throat with a mighty gulp from his tankard.

''Ere, 'ere!' His harangue was greeted by a shout of approval, to be immediately drowned by the angry voices of the dissenters.

'That's what comes of 'avin' a village what's owned by a private individual,' exclaimed a fat florid-faced man dressed in riding-breeches and a rough tweed coat. 'If Owen Winslow 'ad done right with his property he wouldn't have allowed that mortgage to go unpaid afore 'e died, an' now they're foreclosing to sell that patch of land for a factory, an' I say you can't stop 'em!'

A sudden silence greeted his words, and in the midst of it a weedy-looking youth with a cap on the back of his head pushed himself to the front of the crowd.

'I reckon you're all wastin' yer time,' he said. 'Mr. Criller's right. What's the good of talkin'? Whether we want this 'ere factory or not'll make no difference. We ain't got no power to stop it, anyway.'

'That's where you're wrong.' John Tarley, his fine old face crimson with anger, the muscles of his mouth twitching visibly, glared at the speaker with rheumy eyes. 'Why can't we object in a body? Put our case before every man-jack in the village, and raise the money to pay off the mortgage. We could do it bit by bit, an' then we could do what we blamed well liked with the land.'

'How are we goin' to raise five thousand pounds?' demanded the thin-faced man in the cap. ''Ave a bit of sense, Tarley! It's more'n the village could rake up in a century!'

'Besides, the people what 'old the option would want cash down,' broke in the stout farmer, with a coarse-throated laugh. 'You've got bats in the belfry, John Tarley!'

'Oh, 'ave I?' retorted the outraged Mr. Tarley, banging his tankard down on a beer-stained bench and clenching his fists. 'I'm as good a man as you are, Joe Criller — '

'Now then, now then; don't let's 'ave

no trouble,' said the weedy youth, soothingly. 'Fightin' among ourselves won't do no good.'

'Well, tell 'im to keep a civil tongue in 'is 'ead,' growled John Tarley, with a glare at the fat Mr. Criller. 'Somebody's got to make suggestions, ain't they? It ain't no good leavin' it to any o' you. What about this 'ere Jim Winslow, old Winslow's nephew? Stonehurst belongs to 'im now, an' he's comin' to-day to 'ave a look round. I 'eared Dr. Grendon say so. Now, if 'e turns out to be the right sort of feller with a proper attitude towards his tenantry, why shouldn't 'e advance the money in a lump sum and then sell us the land on our own terms?'

He looked round triumphantly from face to face. His listeners glanced at one another and then began arguing amongst themselves. After five minutes the discussion became heated between those who were in favour of the change and the more conservative members of the community. The latter, however, had a clear majority and were all for preparing a demonstration and visiting Jim Winslow the minute he arrived.

'That's right,' nodded John Tarley, finishing his beer at a gulp. 'Now ye'r talkin' sense. But we ought to 'ave a good spokesman — someone as'll know 'ow to put the thing in the right words.'

'What's wrong with you, John?' said Criller, sneeringly.

'Nothin' at all, Joe Criller,' retorted Tarley quickly, 'but I ain't right for this sort o' thing. I ain't got the edication, for one thing,' he frowned; and then a sly look came into his eyes. 'I know 'oo would be the very person. Miss Heyford up at Wood Dene, if she'd do it for us. If this Jim Winslow's a 'uman young chap, then Miss Heyford can 'andle 'im better than the 'ole village put together.'

With the exception of those who were antagonistic the proposal was received with gruff approval. It was decided that a visit should be paid to Wood Dene immediately. John Tarley was to head the expedition, accompanied by his three special satellites — Tim Peak, Sam Bates and Andrew Young. They discussed in detail over fresh tankards of the excellent ale provided by the Crossed Hands exactly what they were going to say. This involved much argument, but eventually everybody was satisfied, and they set off on their errand.

Wood Dene stood on the fringe of the village, an attractive house perched on the brow of a hill overlooking the sea. It was set in two acres of well-kept ground, and as they drew near the drive-gates a certain amount of uneasiness began to make itself evident in the three who accompanied John Tarley. Had they been left to themselves they would probably have turned back at the last minute, but the old man over-ruled their scruples with scathing comments and led the way up the drive. It twisted abruptly just before reaching the house, and as they turned the corner a pretty girl with corn-coloured hair came out from behind a rose-covered pergola to the left of the lawn. She was slim and moved with the easy grace of perfect health. In one of her gloved hands she held a pair of pruning shears, and catching sight of the four rather nervous-looking villagers, came towards them with an expression of surprise.

'Hullo, John,' she said, addressing Tarley. 'What are you doing here? Do you want to see me?'

Four horny and none too clean hands went up and removed four rather battered articles of headgear.

'Beggin' your pardon, Miss Heyford,' began John Tarley, 'I 'ope we ain't disturbin' you, but we was wantin' to 'ave a word with you about a matter what's affectin' the 'ole village.'

The girl's surprised expression deepened.

'I really don't know how I can be of any help, John,' she said. 'What is it all about?'

In halting sentences John Tarley explained the situation.

It was not entirely news to Jill Heyford, who had, as a matter of fact, already discussed the matter with her aunt that morning. But the plan, however, for stopping the factory was naturally entirely fresh to her, and she listened interestedly until John Tarley had finished.

'I don't mind seeing Mr. Winslow when

he arrives and suggesting your plan to him,' she said, 'but I can't guarantee that I'll be successful. It's rather a lot to ask, in a way, and yet I don't see why he shouldn't do it. When does he arrive?'

'To-day, miss,' answered old John promptly.

She frowned and bit gently at her lower lip.

'Very well,' she said at last, 'I'll try and call at Greytower this evening.'

* * *

Greytower was an ancient creeper-covered building standing in its own well-wooded grounds in the centre of the village. Originally it had been an old fort, a glorified edition of one of the Martello Towers which are dotted at intervals all along this part of the Kentish coast. To the original building in the late nineties a new left-hand wing had been added, so that part of the place was comparatively modern. This, together with certain other alterations, had been instituted by a gentleman of foreign extraction, whose business enterprises had resulted in bringing him in so much money that he had bought, not only Greytower, but all the intervening land as far as the sea, which included the entire village of Stonehurst itself.

Unfortunately a few years after he had completed the purchase the war came along and ruined him. He was obliged to sell both the house and the land, and he found a purchaser in Owen Winslow.

Mr. Winslow, an easy-going old man with a passion for solitude, took up his residence at the Tower, and was seldom seen beyond the confines of the grounds, for he never went anywhere or received visitors. He was unmarried and lived alone, the house being run by a Mrs. North and her husband, who acted as housekeeper and butler respectively.

Mr. Winslow had died suddenly. He was found one morning by North, his butler, dead in his bed. The doctor who had been immediately called in had diagnosed heart-failure as the cause. No one had been either surprised or very much interested. To the people in the neighbourhood he had been little more than a name.

But a shock was in store for the inhabitants of Stonehurst. It had been generally taken for granted that Mr. Winslow was a rich man; therefore when it was announced that, apart from Greytower, and the village that went with it, Mr. Winslow's effects were nil, a certain amount of surprise and no little resentment were felt. The final blow, however, was to come when it was learned that shortly before his death Mr. Winslow had mortgaged several acres of land in the heart of the village, and it was this fact which was the cause of the present trouble.

The old man had left a will bequeathing whatever he possessed at the time of his death to his nephew, James Thorpe Winslow, who was discovered to be living abroad in Cape Town, South Africa. The solicitors who were administering the old man's estate cabled him at once, and in reply he sent a message to say that he was leaving for England immediately.

He had in fact arrived in London two

days previously, and after an interview with the solicitors had been on the point of setting off for Stonehurst, when he had run into an old school-friend whom he had not seen for nearly fifteen years.

Ian McWraith had been overjoyed at the meeting. He had himself only recently returned from abroad, and knowing nobody in London, had been beginning to get rather bored. Therefore he regarded Jim Winslow's advent as little more than an act of providence.

McWraith was an enormous man. Seventeen stone of muscle and bone and not an ounce of superfluous fat, he reminded one of a rugged mountain.

When he was angry — which was quite often, because he had one of those tempers which are easily aroused — his massive features became all angles and shadows. In this mood he looked terrible, but ordinarily he had an infectious grin that stretched from ear to ear, and made even his broken nose passable.

His one delight was a fight. If by any chance he could succeed in becoming the central figure in a scrap he was completely happy. No single person had, however, been able to stand up to him for more than five minutes, for his punch was like the kick of an ox.

He had easily persuaded Jim to put off his visit to Stonehurst and spend a couple of days with him in London. Beside his enormous companion Jim Winslow looked rather on the small side. But the comparison was deceptive, for actually he was well above medium height, broad-shouldered and fit as a fiddle. His dark hair contrasted rather alarmingly with McWraith's unruly red patch, and his tanned, clear-cut features made a good foil for the other's rough-hewn face.

On the second day it occurred to Jim that his friend might like to come down with him to Stonehurst. He had already explained the reason that had brought him back to England, and McWraith had been intensely interested. The invitation was accepted promptly, and the pair of them set out with the intention of purchasing a second-hand car which would take them to Jim Winslow's new home. They had succeeded in picking up a bargain, and on the afternoon of the following day started on their journey.

The actual distance from London to Stonehurst was roughly seventy miles, but the car developed tyre trouble before they had travelled fifteen, and dusk was falling when they reached the outskirts of the village.

'This is the place,' said Jim, nodding towards a signpost as they flashed by. 'It looks pretty good to me.'

He eyed the ribbon of white road ahead that merged into the blue-grey dusk of the coming night. An odd cottage here and there raised its thatched roof and smoking chimneys above the green of the surrounding trees; the open fields gave place to flower-filled gardens, and then the road swung to the right and began to slope steeply upwards. The cottages became closer together and intermingled with one or two small shops. They passed a low rambling building of white stone and timber, which, from the sound of voices and the lights that came from within, Jim took to be the village inn. A little farther on were more shops and cottages that straggled away into tall hedges and open fields again, and then a sudden fork in the road, the right-hand arm of which seemed to twist round and lead back the way they had come.

Jim slowed the car until it was barely moving.

'According to my directions,' he said, 'the entrance to the house is about a hundred yards along this right-hand branch.'

He swung the car round as he spoke, increased the speed, and proceeded along the right-hand road, keeping a keen look-out for the drive-gates.

'Well, I shan't be sorry when we get there,' mumbled McWraith, shifting his huge bulk with difficulty in the small seat. 'I'm getting cramped.'

'You shouldn't travel in a car at all,' retorted Jim. 'What you need is a pantechnicon!' and then before the other could reply he added: 'Here we are!' and jerked his head towards the side of the road.

The tall hedge had suddenly bulged inwards, forming a bay, and in the centre were two tall redbrick pillars from which swung elaborate iron gates that were fortunately open.

'Enter the lord of the manor!' said McWraith in a voice which was like the gentle booming of a heavy gun; 'and let's hope he's got a well-stocked larder.'

'According to the solicitors he's got precious little else!' said Jim, with a chuckle, as he ran the car up the tree-lined drive.

Rounding a sharp bend, they came in sight of the house, and as Jim stopped the car before the big door it opened and a man appeared on the top of the steps, silhouetted against the flood of orange light which streamed out from the hall behind him.

He peered at them for a moment and then hurried down the steps, reaching the car just as Jim got out.

'Mr. Winslow?' he enquired, looking quickly from one to the other.

'That's my name,' said Jim. 'Are you North?'

'I'm North, sir,' was the deferential reply. 'Very pleased to welcome you to Greytower, sir.'

Jim thanked him and tried to suppress the sudden and unaccountable dislike which he had taken to this man. Perhaps it was his imagination, but there was something actually repellent about him.

'You got my wire?' he asked as the butler led the way into the house.

'Yes, sir,' North smiled ingratiatingly; 'and I think you'll find everything prepared for you.' He moistened his lips nervously and went on: 'I should like to take this opportunity of saying, sir, that my wife and I would be very happy to continue in your service, providing, of course, that you haven't made other arrangements. We were with your late uncle for fifteen years, and he was quite satisfied, sir.'

'I'm sure he was,' said Jim crisply, and became aware that a woman had entered the hall. A biggish woman with a quiet, firm step. She was standing motionless by the foot of the staircase, watching them from a pair of eyes that were as black as coal.

'This is my wife, sir,' said North deprecatingly.

The woman made a movement that was

half a bow, and half a curtsy, and her swarthy face was completely expressionless.

'I hope you're going to like it here, sir,' she said in a voice that was so low as to be almost inaudible. 'It's a fine old house.'

'I shall be able to see it better in the daylight,' said Jim, and he felt that he liked Mrs. North even less than he liked her husband.

'By the way, this is a friend of mine' — he introduced McWraith — 'he'll be staying here for some time, so will you fix up a room for him?'

Mrs. North eyed the gigantic Scot doubtfully.

'I will do my best, sir,' she said, 'but I don't think there's a bed' — she hesitated — 'that will be big enough.'

'Anything will do for me,' boomed McWraith, waving a huge hand. 'I curl up like a snail!'

He grinned, but no answering smile appeared on the thin lips of the housekeeper. Her face was a mask; not even her eyes gave the slightest indication of her thoughts.

'I will see that a room is prepared,' she

said. 'What time would you like dinner, sir?'

'Just as soon as ever you can get it ready,' said Jim, 'and in the meantime we should like a wash, if you could bring us some hot water.'

'See about it, will you, Alice?' said the butler; and the woman nodded and disappeared through a door at the back of the hall.

'If you'll come this way, sir,' continued North, 'I'll show you to your room.'

He led the way up the broad staircase, on to a square landing and paused half-way along a corridor that ran from it towards the back of the house. Opening a door, he stood aside for Jim to enter.

'I'll go and bring up your luggage, sir,' he said as Jim and McWraith crossed the threshold, and they heard his soft footsteps pad along the corridor and fade away in the distance.

Jim looked round the room interestedly. It was a huge apartment, with two curtained windows that reached from floor to ceiling, and was half-panelled in oak that time had coloured to a rich black. An enormous four-poster bed occupied the centre, its footboard facing the wide old-fashioned fireplace in which a cheerful fire was burning. Above the panelling cream-coloured walls rose to the beamed ceiling. There were no pictures of any kind, and the only touch of modernity was a large easychair that occupied one side of the hearth. It was an austere room, but of a mellow austerity which was not displeasing, and yet as Jim advanced farther into the dim light of the shaded oil-lamp that stood upon a table near the bed, and was the sole means of illumination, he felt suddenly cold. A momentary chill that was like a draught of cold air.

'Well, what do you think of the ancestral home?' asked McWraith.

Jim looked at him, and there was a perceptible pause before he replied.

'I don't know,' he said slowly at length.

'What do you mean?' asked the Scotsman, raising his eyebrows.

'Just what I say,' replied Jim. 'I like it, and — I don't like it. There's something — queer about it.'

'Rubbish!' retorted McWraith. 'You're tired, and you're imagining things. Wait till you've had a good dinner.'

'Don't you find anything strange about the atmosphere of the place?' asked Jim.

'No,' answered his friend. 'It's just the sort of house I like.'

Jim looked at him steadily.

'You're not telling the truth,' he said bluntly. 'You feel the same about it as I do, only you don't like to admit it. I noticed your expression as soon as we got inside the door. There *is* something queer. I don't know if it's this old furniture and all these dusty old trappings, or merely the idea of stepping into a dead man's shoes, but I don't like it, and I don't like that couple down — '

He broke off suddenly, his lips still parted in the act of forming the word 'stairs.'

From somewhere, whether inside or out it was impossible to tell, came a shrill scream. It rose to a howl, quavered down the scale and drifted away to silence.

'What in God's name was that?' muttered Jim, and his face went grey beneath its tan.

2

In the Night

'I trust you were not alarmed, sir,' said the soft voice of North close at hand, and Jim wheeled round.

The butler, a suitcase in either hand, stood watching them from the doorway.

'What was that cry? Did you hear it?' demanded Jim sharply.

'Yes, sir. It was only the dog,' said the butler apologetically. 'I'm sorry if it startled you, sir.' He came noiselessly into the room and set down the bags.

'Oh, I see.' Jim felt vaguely relieved. 'Was that what it was? What's the matter with the dog?'

'Nothing, sir. He sometimes howls like that when he wants to come in,' said the butler with a faint smile. 'It used to startle Mr. Winslow sometimes.'

'I'm not surprised,' remarked Jim. 'It was a horrible din.'

'Yes, sir; I'll do my best to see that it doesn't occur again,' said North. 'I'll go and fetch your hot water now, sir.'

He left the room, closing the door gently behind him, and when he had gone Ian McWraith looked at his friend with a peculiar expression.

'You were quite right about this place being queer,' he said a little grimly, 'and that scream hasn't made it any less queer.'

'Oh, now that we know what it is — ' Jim stopped as the other gave an impatient exclamation.

'You know as well as I do that sound was never made by a dog,' he said quietly. 'That fellow North is a damned liar!'

'What do you think it was, then?' asked Jim.

'I don't know what it was, or what caused it,' said McWraith. 'But I'm willing to bet that it came from a human throat.'

Jim frowned. His friend had put into words the thought that had been in his own mind.

'If that's the case, somebody must have

been having a pretty bad time,' he said uneasily. 'What are we going to do about it?'

'Nothing openly,' growled McWraith, 'but on the quiet we'll keep our eyes skinned.'

He looked round sharply. A faint sound had come from the direction of the door, a faint, almost inaudible click as though someone outside had inadvertently touched the handle.

McWraith took a quick step towards the door, and as he did so the handle clicked again, and this time the door opened and North appeared on the threshold, carrying a large jug of beaten copper.

'Your hot water, sir,' he said, crossing to the washstand and setting it down. 'Dinner will be ready in half an hour.'

'Thank you, North,' said Jim shortly, and after a momentary hesitation the butler withdrew.

'I don't like that fellow, Ian,' said Jim, as he slipped off his jacket and rolled up his shirt-sleeves. 'And I don't like his wife either.'

'Neither do I,' grunted McWraith. 'She reminds me of a snake.'

Jim splashed some of the water into the basin and began to wash his hands.

'We're probably imagining a lot of things that don't exist,' he said. 'Maybe it's coming to a strange house and seeing it for the first time in the dark. Probably to-morrow, in the daylight, when we are less tired, we shall feel different.'

'There was nothing imaginary about that cry,' said McWraith.

Jim laved his face.

'Perhaps it *was* a dog,' he spluttered, grabbing a towel.

'Perhaps,' said his friend, but there was no conviction in his voice. 'Anyway, let's forget all about it, and hope that there's nothing queer about the dinner. I'm as hungry as a starving cat!'

They finished washing and went down to the dining-room, and Jim had to admit that the place looked very pleasant indeed.

A long refectory table was laid for dinner, and in the big open hearth a fire crackled cheerily. In its light the old oak took on a warm hue, reflecting little sparkling points of fire that were enhanced by the six candles that illumined the table.

'Not so bad,' remarked Jim. 'If the dinner is as good as the setting I shall be quite satisfied.'

The dinner was. It was a simple meal, but it was beautifully cooked, and they thoroughly enjoyed it. They had reached the coffee stage when North tapped at the door and entered.

'Excuse me, sir,' he said in an undertone, looking at Jim, 'but Miss Heyford would like to see you.'

'Miss Heyford?' echoed Jim. 'Who the deuce is she?'

'She's a very charming young lady, sir,' answered the butler. 'She lives at Wood Dene on the outskirts of the village.'

Jim glanced at McWraith with a rather bewildered expression, and then back again at the butler.

'What does she want?' he asked.

North smiled faintly.

'I've no idea, sir,' he replied, shaking his head.

'I suppose I'd better see her,' muttered

Jim. 'Have we a drawing-room?'

'Yes, sir,' answered the butler. 'The room facing this one.'

'Show her in there, then,' said Jim, 'and I'll come in a moment.'

The butler went out and Jim rose to his feet.

'You'd better come with me,' he said to McWraith, 'and protect me from the designing females of Stonehurst!'

His friend grinned and followed him to the door.

Jill Heyford was standing in front of the fireplace when they entered the long chintz-hung drawing-room, and Jim mentally decided that the butler had not exaggerated when he had described the visitor as charming. He had never seen anyone quite so dainty as the slim girl who eyed him interestedly as he entered.

'You wished to see me?' he asked.

'Yes, if you are Mr. Winslow,' she replied with a pleasant smile.

'That's my name,' said Jim. 'This is a friend of mine, Mr. McWraith.'

The girl bowed to Ian, and Jim pushed forward a chair.

'Do please sit down, won't you?' he invited.

She sank into the chair with a murmur of thanks, and Jim waited to hear the reason of her visit.

'I must apologise, Mr. Winslow,' she said, 'for disturbing you in this unconventional manner, but I have been asked by several of the villagers to see you, and since I promised I would, here I am.'

Without any further preliminaries she explained her mission and Jim rubbed his chin.

'You've put me in a very awkward position, Miss Heyford,' he admitted frankly. 'I quite see your point of view, or rather the point of view of the people concerned, and I'd be only too pleased to help if I could. Unfortunately, I haven't got five thousand pounds.'

'Oh!' The girl looked at him rather blankly, and then she smiled. 'In that case, of course, nothing can be done. I hope you didn't mind my coming?'

'Not in the least,' said Jim hastily, 'I'm only sorry that I can't do something. I tell you what, though,' he added, 'I'll go into the matter thoroughly and if I can think of any way in which I can help you I will.'

She thanked him and half rose from her chair.

'Please don't go unless you must,' said Jim. 'You see, you may be able to help me a little now you're here. You know all about the place and that sort of thing. What are the people like around here, and what does everybody do?'

'They're mostly farmers,' she explained, 'and just ordinary villagers. Of course, there are a few others. There's Dr. Grendon, and Mr. Toogood, and Mr. and Mrs. Gordon-Watts. They live at the White House at the end of the High Street; you must have passed it on your way from London.'

'I remember it,' put in McWraith. 'Rather a pretty place with a lot of flowering creeper. Is that where you mean?'

She nodded.

'Then there's Mr. Lucia, who's just rented the Martins' cottage for six months, and Mr. Japper, who owns the Crossed Hands. He's very popular in the village.'

'Crossed Hands?' said Jim. 'That must

be the inn we passed.'

'It's the original inn,' she said, 'where the smugglers who infested these parts, I don't know how many hundreds of years ago, used to hide. There are lots of places like that around here. Stonehurst might almost be called a slice of the past. Are you thinking of staying here permanently?'

'I don't know,' replied Jim. 'It all depends.'

'I asked because, if you do, you're sure to meet all these people,' she went on. 'They're a funny crowd — some of them. I think you'll like it here, at least — ' she hesitated, reddened and added hastily, 'at least you're sure to.'

Neither Jim nor Ian McWraith missed that sudden intake of breath and the momentary embarrassment that had accompanied it. Jim was convinced that the girl had not ended her sentence as she had at first intended. He made no comment, however, and she was so obviously anxious to cover up that momentary slip that she changed the subject quickly and went on chatting about Stonehurst and its inhabitants.

Suddenly, almost in the midst of a sentence, she stopped and looked at her watch with a start of surprise.

'I'd no idea it was so late,' she said in dismay, getting up quickly. 'My aunt will be wondering what has become of me. I really must go.'

She said good-bye to McWraith, and Jim took her to the door. When he came back he found his friend smoking a cigarette in front of the fireplace, his mouth expanded in a wide smile.

'That's what I call a really pretty girl,' remarked McWraith. 'You ought to be jolly glad you've got neighbours like that. If there are any more of the same brand I've a good mind to come and stop here permanently myself.'

'I wish you would,' said Jim fervently. 'I don't much fancy stopping here alone.'

'I'll think about it,' replied his friend. 'It looks to me as if it might be interesting.'

'What about having a look round the place?' suggested Jim. 'We haven't seen much of it so far.'

'An excellent idea,' agreed McWraith, 'and perhaps our friend the butler can be persuaded to show us that extraordinary dog that screams when it wants to come in.'

He looked across at Jim with a queer expression on his face.

'What are you getting at?' asked Jim, as he crossed the room and touched the bell.

'I'm not getting at anything,' replied McWraith. 'I'm just curious, that's all.'

Jim had to ring twice before North answered the summons, and when the man did come he was breathing heavily as though he had been running.

He offered an explanation for this, which was also an apology.

'I'm very sorry, sir,' he said. 'My wife told me you had rung twice. I was down in the cellar getting some coal.'

'That's all right,' said Jim, but his eyes narrowed slightly as he noticed that the butler's coat was sprinkled here and there with moisture that glistened in the light.

'Your cellars must be very damp,' remarked McWraith, and North's pasty face went a shade paler.

'I — I had to go out to the outhouse as well, sir,' he said hastily, with a glance at his wet coat sleeve, 'to get some logs. We don't keep them in the cellar, sir.'

It was a plausible explanation, and Jim was rather annoyed with himself when he found his mind rejecting it. And yet he did reject it, and would have been willing to bet a considerable sum that North was not speaking the truth.

'What was it you wanted, sir?' asked the butler, darting quick glances from one to the other.

'We thought,' said Jim, 'that we'd rather like to look over the place. Will you show us round?'

The butler's hesitation before he replied was only momentary.

'Certainly, sir, if you wish,' he said, 'though I don't think you'll be able to see very much tonight.'

'What we miss to-night,' said Jim, 'we can see in the morning.'

'Very good, sir,' answered North. 'If you'll wait here for a moment I'll get a lantern.'

He glided away with the peculiar cat-like tread that was a characteristic of the man.

Jim looked at his friend.

'You don't believe he'd been in the cellar, either,' he said, and it was a statement rather than a question.

'I don't believe anything about the man at all,' answered McWraith candidly. 'He may be a confoundedly good butler, but he's a darned sight better liar. Did you notice his boots?'

Jim shook his head.

'They were caked with mud,' said McWraith. 'Caked with it! Unless the outhouse is a couple of miles away he couldn't have got in that state getting logs.'

Jim's brows met in a troubled frown.

'Then what *was* he doing?' he demanded.

McWraith shrugged his shoulders.

'I don't know,' he replied, 'but there's something deuced queer going on. I — '

'If you're ready, sir,' said the soft voice of North, and Jim swung round quickly to find the butler standing in the open doorway with a lighted hurricane lantern in his hand.

If he had heard McWraith's remark he gave no sign. Perhaps he had not. Perhaps he had only just arrived when he had spoken, for both their backs had been turned towards the door, and neither had heard him approach.

'We're ready,' said Jim shortly, and the butler led the way out into the hall.

'I suppose it's the older parts of the house you would like to see, sir,' he said, and Jim agreed.

He conducted them along a passage leading off the hall and, opening a door, ushered them into a large stone kitchen. A crackling fire was burning in a big open fireplace, and at a massive table Mrs. North was ironing placidly. She gave them a quick glance as they passed through, followed it with a jerky little bow, and went on impassively with her work.

'This, sir,' said North, 'is part of the old fortifications, though Mr. Winslow had a lot of alterations made.'

He crossed over to a solid-looking door and, taking a key from his pocket, unlocked it. Beyond was a dark passageway, and the butler explained that this led to the tower. There was a similar door at the other end of the passage which was unlocked, and passing through this, they found themselves at the base of the squat tower which gave the house its name. It had apparently been used as a lumber-room, for several empty packing-cases were piled in one corner and near them was a broken chair from which the stuffing had tumbled out on to the floor. Reared against one wall were the remains of an iron bedstead, red with rust. An unusual-looking object attracted Jim's attention, and he went over and examined it. It was a framework of enamelled iron, supported on four rubber-tyred wheels, and resembled the type of ambulance used in hospitals for taking patients into the operating-theatre.

'How did you come by that?' he asked, for the contraption appeared to be quite new.

'Mr. Winslow bought it about a year ago, sir,' replied North. 'He suffered from rheumatism very badly, and was sometimes quite unable to stand. On these occasions I used to wheel him into the garden.'

'I see,' said Jim.

'Surely,' put in McWraith, 'an ordinary bath-chair would have been more convenient?'

'I suggested that at the time, sir,' said North respectfully, 'but Mr. Winslow was, if you'll excuse me saying so, sir, a very self-willed gentleman.'

'Where does that lead to?' asked Jim, pointing to a door under the spiral stone staircase that led to the upper regions of the tower.

'I don't know, sir,' said North. 'So far as I can remember it has always been locked, and I have never seen the key.'

McWraith strolled over and examined it.

'Why, it's iron!' he said, and, gripping the handle, shook it violently.

The door, however, fitted closely, and except for a slight rattle, remained immovable.

'Funny place to put a door like that,' said Jim. 'I wonder what's behind it?'

'I think, sir,' answered North at his elbow, 'that there must be some sort of small room built in the thickness of the wall. I've never seen it; it was locked when Mr. Winslow first came to the house, and we've never been able to open it. Would you like to see the rest of the tower, sir?'

Jim said he would, and North began to ascend the worn stone staircase, lighting the way with his lantern, which cast long flickering shadows, and really did more to accentuate the gloom than to serve as an illuminant.

The tower consisted of four square rooms built one over the other. At regular intervals narrow slit-like apertures acted as windows. These were unglazed, and the wind blowing through them made a peculiar whistling, moaning sound that was extraordinarily eerie. There was nothing in any of the rooms except dust, and without pausing they went on towards the top of the tower. From here they could see across the intervening land to the sea, and in spite of the drizzle of rain that was falling they both remained for some time. Far away out to sea twinkled the orange light of an anchored lightship, and farther to the west the intermittent light of the Dungeness lighthouse. It flashed, went out, and flashed again.

'The view from here in the daytime must be magnificent,' muttered McWraith, standing by his friend's side, and Jim nodded absently.

He was counting the time lapse between those intermittent flashes.

'Ten seconds,' he said below his breath, and although he had no particular reason for noting the fact then, later he was to be very glad that he had done so.

There was nothing more to be seen in the tower, and they returned to the kitchen. Mrs. North was still ironing methodically, and this time she gave no indication whatever that she was aware of their presence.

The butler took them down a narrow flight of stairs and showed them the cellars, which were extensive and more like dungeons. There was a coal cellar and a well-stocked wine cellar, but for the most part they were unused. By the time they had seen these Jim was feeling tired and announced his intention of postponing further exploration until the morning.

They returned to the drawing-room, and were in the midst of a final cigarette when North came in with a tray containing whisky, soda and glasses.

'Excellent!' boomed McWraith. 'I can just do with a spot before turning in.'

North asked if they wanted anything further, and on receiving a negative reply wished them 'Good night' and retired.

McWraith poured himself out a generous peg, and looked enquiringly at Jim, who shook his head.

'No whisky, thanks,' he said. 'I'll have a drop of soda though.'

In the corridor outside his bedroom they found Mrs. North waiting.

'I've put Mr. McWraith in the room next to yours, sir,' she said. 'The linen has been well aired, and there's fresh water in the jug.'

'Thank you,' said Jim. 'Good night, Mrs. North.'

'Good night, sir,' said the woman. 'I hope you both sleep well.'

'I think I shall sleep very well,' said McWraith with a prodigious yawn as she disappeared in the shadows of the staircase. 'I don't think I've ever felt so tired before.'

Jim went with him to his room, saw that he had everything that he required, and then came back to his own and went to bed.

But for some reason or other he did not sleep. The wind had risen and he could hear it moaning round the house, and fainter and far away the noise of the surf on the beach. For some time he lay listening, twisting and turning from side to side, and then, hoping that perhaps a cigarette would soothe his nerves and make sleep more possible, he got up.

A fitful, watery moon was shining, and its light faintly lit the room. Without troubling to light the lamp, he searched for, and found, his cigarettes, lit one, and, strolling over to the window, looked out.

From where he stood he could see the tower rising blackly against the sky, and as he looked something attracted and held his attention — something that was moving in the shadows of the base of the huge stone structure. It was a curious, shapeless thing, and seemed to be gliding along the path that led away from the house.

He craned forward interestedly, wondering what it could be, and then, as he watched with quickened breath, it came out of the shadows for an instant into the pale light of the moon.

The cigarette dropped from his fingers as he stared incredulously at what he saw.

Somebody was pushing the wheeled-ambulance, and on it, plainly visible in the moonlight, the white face upturned to the sky, was the body of a man!

3

Shadgold Asks a Favour

Mr. Trevor Lowe flung down the book he had been reading with an exclamation of disgust and began to stuff tobacco into the bowl of his pipe.

His secretary, Arnold White, looked across from the desk at which he was working.

'What's the matter?' he inquired. 'Book a bad one?'

The dramatist sniffed savagely.

'Quite well written for its type,' he replied. 'It's the type I complain of. There isn't a solitary character in it who isn't cross and nasty. They've all got kinks of some sort or another, and they spend pages analysing themselves to find out what they are, and pages more to find out why they've got them!'

White smiled, and twisting round in his chair, glanced at the cover.

'It had very good reviews,' he remarked.

'I've no doubt it did,' answered Lowe, striking a match. 'It's sufficiently gloomy to have been eulogised by every newspaper in the country! It's the type of literature that I call really pernicious. I suppose it can be classed under the heading of a slice of life, and to a certain extent it may be, but taking the world as a whole, it only portrays a crumb. You cannot tell me that the people characterised in such a book as that' — he jerked his head contemptuously at the novel lying on the settee — 'are true of the majority. The world is made up mostly of decent hard-working people, who are much too busy earning their bread and butter to worry about inhibitions. Why, then, with such a large selection to choose from, should these authors pick on a small minority to write about?'

'Presumably,' said the secretary, 'because there is a demand for that kind of story.'

'There is a demand for any story, provided it is sufficiently talked about,' retorted Trevor Lowe. 'It's becoming increasingly common for people to do and read and think what somebody else tells them they ought to do, read, and think. They don't read a book for the enjoyment they are going to get out of it, but for the enjoyment they are going to get talking to Mrs. Smith or Jones or Brown *about* it. It's the correct thing to have read it, so they rush to their library and demand it. I don't say that this is true of everybody; a great number of people choose their reading matter because it gives them pleasure, and for one hour or two makes them forget all the worries, big and little, that go to make up their lives.'

He paused for a moment and puffed furiously at his pipe.

'There was one time not so very long ago,' he continued, 'when the penny dreadful was cited as responsible for a great deal of trouble. A boy was found stealing the jam, or injuring property, or getting into some very ordinary mischief, and the penny dreadful was blamed. A youth got into bad company and stole the petty cash, and again it was the penny dreadful that was at the bottom of it. But the penny dreadful never has and never will be responsible for so much crime, misery and disaster as these so-called psychological novels.

'Think of the effect on the youth of the country of a book like that' — he swept his arm towards the offending novel — 'the people who are just reaching adolescence. They dig down into their subconsciousness and try to discover things that don't exist, and never did exist, and they end up after a long dose of this 'nothing-is-worth-while' creed by looking out of the window on a bright spring morning and deciding there's nothing left to live for. It's taught them self-analysis in the wrong way. It's taught them — '

He broke off as there came a tap on the door, and the housekeeper entered.

'Inspector Shadgold has called, sir,' she announced. 'What shall I tell him?'

'Oh, ask him to come in,' said Lowe quickly, and the woman departed.

'I wonder what *he* wants,' said White. 'It's ages since we've seen him, isn't it?'

'He's been away for his holiday,' replied Lowe. 'No doubt that accounts for it.'

Apparently the holiday had done the inspector good, for when he entered his face was redder than ever, and the secretary thought that his waist-line had decidedly expanded.

'Hullo, Mr. Lowe,' he jerked, throwing his hard bowler hat on to a chair. 'I hope I'm not intruding?'

'Only too glad to see you, Shadgold,' said the dramatist. 'Did you have a good time?'

'Eh?' Shadgold looked at him in surprise, and then: 'Oh, you mean the holiday? Yes, it was all right — while it lasted.'

'You'll have to start dieting now you're back,' said White with a grin.

Shadgold glared at him.

'What do you mean — while it lasted?' asked Lowe hastily.

'Well, by rights I should still be away, Mr. Lowe,' answered the inspector. 'But I was recalled yesterday.'

'Oh, I see,' murmured the dramatist. 'Well, sit down, my dear fellow, and tell us all the news.'

'Thanks.' The Scotland Yard man

perched himself on the arm of a chair. 'As a matter of fact, Mr. Lowe,' he went on, 'I've come round to ask you a favour.'

A slight smile twitched the corners of the dramatist's lips. He had guessed from the inspector's manner that the call was not entirely a friendly one.

'Go ahead,' he said. 'What is it?'

'Do you remember my telling you about a man called Locker?' asked Shadgold abruptly, and Lowe frowned.

'Locker?' he repeated. 'No, I can't say that I do.'

'You must remember, surely,' said the inspector. 'I believe I introduced him to you once. He was quite a clever fellow, except that he would talk. Whenever he had successfully concluded a case he used to talk about it for hours on end. We nicknamed him the 'Loud Speaker' at the Yard. Now do you remember him?'

'Why, yes, I seem to have some vague recollection about whom you're talking,' answered the dramatist.

'Well,' continued Shadgold, 'he went after Canning, the forger, two years ago, and completely disappeared.'

'Now I remember,' said Lowe, and he looked interested. 'What about it?'

'Well' — Shadgold gave his chair a hitch and leaned forward, his hands on his knees — 'if you remember, he was never found, neither he nor Canning, and the general theory at the time was that he had accepted a heavy bribe from Canning to let him get away, then got frightened and cleared off himself.'

'Yes, I remember discussing it with you,' said Lowe, 'and suggesting that it was equally possible that Canning might have killed him and concealed the body. But what's all this got to do with the favour you want to ask me?'

Shadgold cleared his throat and fidgeted for a moment.

'It's got a great deal to do with it,' he said. 'Two months ago Lew Telmann did a 'bust' at Hennigers, the jeweller's, in Bond Street, and got away with over eighty thousand pounds worth of emeralds which they'd got specially to show a customer. We knew it was Telmann by the way the job had been done, and we sent two men to go and pull him in, but he'd left all his usual haunts, and they couldn't trace him. Six weeks ago, however, news came through that he'd been seen in Kent, just outside Hythe. We sent two fellers, Roach and Scory, down to follow up the clue, and from that day to this there hasn't been a sign of them.'

The dramatist sat forward in his chair, and from his expression was interested.

'Do you mean that they disappeared?' he asked.

'Completely,' declared Shadgold. 'We searched the whole neighbourhood, but there was not a trace of them anywhere.'

'Extraordinary!' muttered Lowe.

'That's not all,' went on the inspector. 'Three weeks ago — while I was on my holiday — there was some trouble with a car at Oxford Circus. It was travelling too fast and failed to stop when the man on point duty tried to pull it up. He took the number, however, and we communicated with the police at Hythe, and they sent a summons to the owner of the car, a Mr. Gordon-Watts, who lived at an adjoining village called Stonehurst. The Hythe police were very busy at the time. There'd been an outbreak of assaults in the district: women crossing lonely places were knocked down and their handbags pinched; and every available local man was out searching for the assailants. One of our fellows — a plain-clothes man called Drin — was down there making an inquiry on some other business altogether, and as he had to pass through Stonehurst on his way back, he offered to serve the summons and save the local superintendent calling one of his men off the chase. Drin left Hythe at ten o'clock in the morning, but he never arrived at Mr. Gordon-Watts', and nobody's seen him since. Like Locker, Roach and Scory, he's vanished into thin air.'

'This is extraordinarily interesting,' said Lowe. 'Do you think there is a connection between these disappearances?'

'The Assistant-Commissioner thinks so,' answered Shadgold. 'And that's why my holiday has been cut short. I've been given the job of finding out exactly what *has* happened to these men.'

'And I presume,' said Lowe with a twinkle in his eye, 'since you've come round here, that you want me to help you.'

'That's right, Mr. Lowe,' replied Shadgold. 'I know you're interested in this sort of thing, particularly if it's something out of the ordinary; and this is out of the ordinary enough, God knows!'

'Well, what can I do?' asked the dramatist.

'Well,' answered the inspector a little hesitantly, 'you see, it's like this. Roach and Scory went to Hythe and disappeared. We don't know where Locker went to, but Hythe seems to me to be the place to concentrate on. Whatever happened to Drin must have happened quite close to Hythe, because Stonehurst's only about ten miles away, and from all accounts he never reached there. Now, what I'd like you to do, if you'll be kind enough to do it, is to go down to Hythe and have a nose round. There's something queer going on in the neighbourhood, and I think you're more likely to find out what it is than I am. For one thing, you don't look like a policeman and I do; and for another, I've got an idea that whatever it is that's at the bottom of this business, it's something pretty big. If you're too busy, don't mind saying so — '

'As a matter of fact I'm not very busy at the moment,' answered Lowe. 'I've finished my new play, and it doesn't go into rehearsal for another month.'

'Then you'll take it on?' said the inspector eagerly.

The dramatist nodded.

'I'll do my best,' he said. 'I'll go down tomorrow and see what I can find out. Mind you, I can't promise that I'll be successful.'

'That's awfully good of you, Mr. Lowe,' said Shadgold gratefully. 'Now, is there anything more you want to know?'

'I don't think so.' Trevor Lowe shook his head. 'I suppose you've got official reports concerning the disappearances of these men, with all the details such as dates, times, etc.?'

'Yes, we've got all those,' said Shadgold. 'Do you want 'em?'

'I'd like you to send them round first thing in the morning if you could manage it,' said the dramatist.

'I can do better than that,' said the

inspector, glancing at his watch. 'I can let you have them this evening. I'm going back to the Yard now, and I'll send them straight up.'

'That's fine,' said Lowe. 'What about a drink before you go?'

'It will have to be a quick one,' said Shadgold; 'I've got to get back in time to catch the Assistant-Commissioner before he leaves.'

Arnold White went over to a side-table and mixed him a stiff whisky and soda, and he drank half of it at a gulp.

'You'll keep in touch with me — won't you, Mr. Lowe?' he said. 'Whether you discover anything or not.'

'I will,' promised the dramatist; 'I'll drop you a line and let you know what progress we're making.'

Shadgold finished the remainder of his drink, and picked up his hat.

'Well, then I'll say good-bye,' he said, holding out his hand. 'And thanks once more.'

He shook hands with Lowe, nodded to White, and they heard his heavy footsteps hurrying along the passage. The front door slammed and the dramatist turned to his secretary.

'Well?' he said.

'Well?' said White.

'That was a queer story of Shadgold's,' remarked Lowe. 'What do you think of it?'

'I don't think anything of it,' replied Arnold White. 'It's certainly peculiar, these fellows disappearing like that, but I can't think of any reasonable suggestion to account for it.'

'All Scotland Yard men,' said Lowe musingly. 'H'm! I wonder what's behind it.'

White wrinkled his brows.

'The only thing that I can think of,' he said, 'is that these chaps must have stumbled on to something that somebody didn't want them to know anything about.'

'It sounds a little involved the way you put it,' agreed Lowe, 'but I think the same. The question is, what did they stumble on? It must have been something very extraordinary, for Locker disappeared two years ago, and it was not until six weeks ago that the same thing happened to Roach and Scory, and three weeks ago that Drin left Hythe at ten o'clock one morning and was never seen again. That means that this thing, whatever it is, which they accidentally discovered has been going on for at least two years, and possibly longer. I don't mind admitting that I'm very interested. The unusualness of it appeals to me.'

Crime was Trevor Lowe's hobby. During the writing of a mystery play he had sought permission from Scotland Yard to study police methods, and had been turned over to Detective-Inspector Shadgold. At that time the papers were full of the murder of Thomas Carraway, the ex-Member of Parliament, who had been found stabbed to death in the grounds of his house in the country. Shadgold was in charge of the case, and he had suggested that Lowe would acquire all the knowledge he wanted if he accompanied him on his investigations. The dramatist had eagerly agreed, and his help had been so valuable that the Chief-Commissioner himself had written a personal letter of thanks. A friendship had sprung up between himself and the Scotland Yard detective, and since then Shadgold had been in the habit of enlisting his aid on more than one occasion.

Nine o'clock brought a messenger from Scotland Yard with the official reports that the inspector had promised, and Trevor Lowe settled himself in an easy chair in front of the fire, and with the folders on his knee, began to read carefully through them. Except for the fact that they were couched in official language, and that the date and times were set down in detail, he found that there was very little more information to be gathered than Shadgold had already told him.

He was in the middle of the last pages when the telephone bell rang. Arnold White went over to the instrument, and lifted the receiver.

'Hullo!' he called . . . 'Yes . . . Yes . . . Who is that? . . . I don't know. I'll see.'

Covering the mouthpiece with his

hand, he turned to Lowe.

'Somebody wants to speak to you,' he said. 'It's a man, but he won't give his name.'

'Ask him what it's all about,' said the dramatist.

White repeated his remark to the unknown at the other end of the wire.

There was a pause while the caller argued, and then the secretary once more turned.

'He says it's very urgent, and he must speak to you personally,' he reported. 'He sounds to me as if he was scared.'

With an impatient exclamation Lowe laid the typescript he was reading aside, and rose to his feet. Going over to the telephone, he took the receiver from White's hand and held it to his ear.

'This is Trevor Lowe speaking,' he said. 'What do you want? Who are you?'

The voice that replied was faint and far away.

'I want to see you, Mr. Lowe,' it said rapidly. 'I *must* see you.'

'Who are you?' repeated the dramatist.

'I can't tell you,' answered the voice. 'I

can't tell you anything on the telephone. Somebody may hear. Can you come down to Stonehurst — now?'

Lowe started.

'Stonehurst?' he said. 'Is that where you're speaking from?'

'Yes,' answered the unknown caller. 'I'm at a call-office. I've got some information, important information, Mr. Lowe, and I must see you. Can you meet me at one o'clock to-night?'

'Where?' asked the dramatist.

'Here,' said the voice. 'There are four crossroads just outside the village with a signpost. On one of the arms you'll see 'Stonehurst three-quarters of a mile.' Meet me there.'

Lowe hesitated.

'If you'll tell me who you are — ' he began, and the other interrupted him.

'You know me,' he said impatiently, and then: 'For God's sake come! There's devilish work going on! I can't tell you any more now; I daren't tell you any more now. There are two men following me. They've got a car outside the Crossed — ' The voice broke off with a gasp.

'All right,' said Lowe, suddenly making up his mind; 'I'll be at the cross-roads at one o'clock.'

There was a click at the other end and the wire went dead.

Coming back to the fireplace, Lowe gave White a rapid account of the conversation.

'Are you going,' asked the secretary. 'It may be a hoax.'

'Hoax or not, I think we ought to go,' replied the dramatist. 'Particularly after what Shadgold told us this evening.'

Arnold White looked at him, a peculiar expression in his eyes.

'By Jove,' he muttered; 'you mean — '

'I mean,' said Lowe seriously, 'that call came from Stonehurst, and it was in the neighbourhood of Stonehurst that Roach, Scory and Drin disappeared!'

4

Death at the Crossroads

Trevor Lowe's sectional motoring-map showed that the quickest way to Stonehurst was by the main road which ran through Wrotham, Maidstone, Ashford, and from thence on to Hythe. There was a secondary road which branched off at Ashford and led on to New Romney, which was not very far from Stonehurst, but the dramatist decided to go on to Hythe and then take the road along the coast.

The night was fine when they left Portland Place, but at Maidstone they ran into a drizzle of rain, and this continued for the rest of the journey.

It was a quarter past twelve when they came into Hythe, with the screen-wiper working furiously, and, veering sharply to the right just outside the town, continued along the main road to Dymchurch.

Lowe decreased his speed considerably here, searching the road ahead for the side turning that would take them up to Stonehurst. He found it, a secondary road that twisted and turned and eventually brought them to a point where it was bisected by another and narrower thoroughfare, at the junction of which stood a four-armed signpost.

'I think this is the place,' said the dramatist as he ran the car into the side of the road and brought it to a halt.

As he spoke a clock somewhere in the distance chimed the three-quarters, and he confirmed the time by a glance at his watch.

'We've got a quarter of an hour to wait,' he said, and taking his pipe and tobacco pouch from his pocket, he filled the former and lit it.

The rain was still falling in a thin, wetting drizzle, and the gentle noise that it made on the leaves and hedges surrounding them was the only sound that broke the stillness of the night. The slight wind that was blowing brought with it a tang of the sea that smelt very clean and fresh after the petrol-laden atmosphere of London. There was no moon, and the clouded sky obscured the stars, so that except for the light from the car the darkness was intense.

They waited in silence while the time crept on, Lowe smoking throughtfully and Arnold White speculating as to what the information was that the unknown man they had come all this way to meet had to reveal.

Presently the same clock that had chimed before struck one, and Lowe sat up a little more alertly in his seat and peered ahead at the dim outline of the signpost. Two minutes went by — five, but there was no sign of the man who had telephoned. Nothing stirred in the darkness of the night, and no sound of approaching footsteps broke the monotonous hiss of the gently falling rain.

The clock struck again, a quarter past one, and Lowe began to get a little impatient. Had the whole thing been a hoax, and was the joker at the moment laughing to himself at having tricked them into making this night journey for nothing? If it had been, there had been very little point in it, and remembering the urgency of the voice, the dramatist was not inclined to believe this explanation.

If it was not a hoax, then something must have happened to the unknown man to keep him from his appointment, or — and this was a possible suggestion — they had come to the wrong place.

With a word to his secretary, Lowe got out of the car and walked towards the signpost. The headlights were shining full on it, and it was quite easy to read the black lettering on the arms. The one pointing directly ahead in the opposite direction from which they had come bore the inscription 'Stonehurst three-quarters of a mile.'

There was little doubt, then, that this was the right place. Lowe walked back to the car, deciding that he would wait until two and then give it up. If anything had happened to detain the man, an hour's grace should surely give him ample time to put in an appearance. There was, of course, always the possibility that he had changed his mind — that something had occurred after the telephone call to prevent him imparting the urgent information which he possessed.

However, it was useless speculating. If the man turned up, all well and good, if not, well, they could do nothing except make the best of a bad job and go back to town.

The time crept slowly on — half-past one, a quarter to two, two — and still nothing happened. As the last notes of the hour were carried away on the wind the dramatist uttered an impatient exclamation and got back into the car.

'I don't think it's any good waiting any longer,' he said. 'We may as well go back.'

White grunted disgustedly.

'We might just as well have stopped at home,' he said. 'As it is we've lost nearly a whole night's sleep for nothing.'

'It can't be helped,' said Lowe philosophically. 'But I should very much like to know what went wrong. I'm convinced the fellow, whoever he was, was genuine.'

He kicked the self-starter, and as the engine purred to life, let in the clutch, and they began to move slowly forward.

'If we go round the island with the signpost,' he said, 'we can turn right round and go back the way we came.'

He carried out the suggestion, and as the car rounded the irregular piece of grass in the centre of the cross-roads the headlights shone brilliantly on a hedge at the side of the road. With a sudden startled cry Arnold White gripped his employer's arm.

'Look there!' he exclaimed hoarsely, and pointed.

Lowe looked, and the next second had jammed on the brakes and brought the car to a skidding standstill.

Below the hedge, so clearly seen in the brilliant light of the headlamps, was a wide ditch, and protruding from this and resting on the grassy edge was a hand!

Lowe jumped out of the car almost before it stopped and ran towards this gruesome sight, and then he saw that the hand belonged to a man who lay in the few inches of water at the bottom of the ditch. His face was visible, and the eyes, glassy and immovable, stared up into the dark arch of the sky. It only needed a glance to show that he was dead, and the round hole in the centre of his forehead, from which the blood had trickled and dried on his white face, amply testified to the manner in which he had met his end.

'What is it?' asked White breathlessly as he hurried up.

'It's either murder or suicide,' answered the dramatist grimly. 'This fellow's been shot through the head.'

With a horrified exclamation the secretary peered down at the lifeless thing in the ditch.

'Good God!' he exclaimed, and stopped abruptly, staring at the sprawling body.

'Not a pleasant sight, is it?' remarked Lowe. 'There's a torch in the right-hand side door-pocket of the car. Will you get it?'

He stood looking down at the man in the ditch while White went on his errand, and when the secretary returned took the torch from his hand, and switching on the powerful white ray, directed it on the dead man.

He was of middle age and shabbily dressed; the brown suit he wore was old and creased, and there was a small slit in one of his brown shoes. His shirt and collar were of a bluish grey and none too clean. His face was thin and lined, and his hair, for he wore no hat, was of a light straw colour. It was not a prepossessing face; the chin was weak and the forehead low and narrow, the eyes set too closely to the broad, rather shapeless, nose. Lowe thought there was something rather familiar about the man, but though he tried hard he couldn't place him. He made a rapid search of the ditch in the vicinity of the body, but there was no sign of the weapon by which the man had met his death. There was the possibility of course that it might be underneath him, but the dramatist thought it advisable not to move the body until the police had seen it and the police doctor had made his examination.

'Take the car, White,' he said, turning to his secretary, 'and find the nearest police station — it's in Hythe, I think — tell them what has happened, and ask them to come back here at once. I'll wait with this fellow till you return.'

White obeyed and, standing in the darkness by the side of the ditch, Lowe watched him swing the car round and drive off in the direction of Hythe. As the red eye of the tail-lamp disappeared in the distance he turned his attention once more to the dead man. This must be the man who had put through that urgent call to Portland Place, demanding to see him; and if he were, it looked a great deal more like murder than suicide. There was no satisfactory reason why the man should have gone to all the trouble and then shot himself before keeping the appointment. But there was every reason why somebody else should have killed him. He had said that he had important information to impart. What this information was Lowe had not the least idea; but if it was concerned with a crime of some description and involved somebody else, then here was a very good motive for the man being killed before he could pass his knowledge on.

The dramatist knelt down beside the motionless form and, taking the greatest care not to disturb the position of the body, went through all the pockets.

They were all empty, and he frowned. This pointed still further to murder, for it is very unusual for any man to walk about with completely empty pockets, and it was unlikely that this particular man should be an exception to the general rule. Whatever he had had on him at the time of his death, therefore, had been removed, and it was not unreasonable to suppose that it had been removed by the person who had killed him.

Lowe was certain now that this was a case of murder — certain that the man before him had been killed in order to keep his mouth shut. But what had he known? What was the vital information that had caused him to ring up Lowe so urgently and arrange that night appointment at the cross-roads? Was it connected with the disappearances? Had this man stumbled on the truth that lay behind the vanishing of Locker, Roach, Scory and Drin? Lowe thought that it was more than possible; it seemed too much of a coincidence to think otherwise. Somewhere in the vicinity of this peaceful countryside there was devilish work going on. Locker had got an inkling of it, and disappeared. Roach, Scory and Drin had followed him, and now this man who had also known something had died before he could speak.

Lowe walked slowly up and down on the edge of the ditch in the darkness and the gently falling rain, his hands thrust deep into the pockets of his overcoat, his brows drawn together in a thoughtful frown.

What was the thing behind it all? Shadgold had said it was something pretty big. But what? What gigantic plot was being hatched in this rural setting? Whatever it was, it had been going on for two years, for it was two years ago that Locker had vanished for good from the sight of his fellow-men. Had these Scotland Yard men, like the man in the ditch, been killed too? Their bodies had never been found, but that was by no means proof that they were still alive.

The dramatist looked round him into the blackness and silence of the countryside. There must be numberless places in the neighbourhood where a man could lie buried without much risk of ever being found.

He was still trying to form some conjecture as to what the thing could be that lay at the root of the mystery when the whine of a car came to his ears, and looking up, he saw the headlights coming towards him. They widened out as they came nearer, and he saw that behind them was a second pair less brilliant than the first.

The car came to a halt by the side of the signposts, and Arnold White got out, followed by a short thick-set man and a uniformed constable.

'This is Superintendent Hartley,' explained the secretary, introducing the newcomer.

'Pleased to meet you, sir,' said the thick-set man. 'There's been pretty bad trouble here, I understand?'

Lowe gave him a brief and concise account of the finding of the dead man, and when he had finished the superintendent went over and peered down at the body.

'Before we go any further,' he said, 'we'd better get the doctor's opinion.' He turned and called into the darkness. 'Are you there, Doctor?'

'Coming,' said a voice, and a little man carrying a black bag appeared in the ray of the car's headlights.

'This is Dr. Peters, our police doctor,' said Hartley as he came up and introduced Lowe.

The doctor grunted, but made no other acknowledgment of the introduction. He was a man of medium height with stooping shoulders, and the owner of an unusually long and skinny neck that protruded from a collar several sizes too large for him. His eyes were pale blue and watery, and he had a habit of sniffing every few minutes as though suffering from a perpetual cold.

The superintendent took him over to the dead man in the ditch, and after staring down at him for a second or two, the doctor dropped on to one knee.

'Give me a little more light, will you?' he said sharply, and Lowe added the light of his own torch to that of Hartley's.

Dr. Peters' examination did not last long.

'He died from a bullet wound in the head,' he announced, rising to his feet. 'It was fired at close range, and has passed right through the brain, making its exit at the base of the skull.'

'Can you tell us approximately how long the man has been dead?' asked Hartley.

The doctor pursed his lips.

'What's the time now?' he asked, and supplied the answer to his question by looking at his watch. 'H'm! Twenty minutes past three. I should say he met his death somewhere between eleven and twelve. It's impossible to tell within an hour or so, but he's certainly been dead for over three hours. I can't be more accurate at the moment. There'll have to be a post mortem, of course, and then I'll be able to tell you more about it.'

'You say there was nothing in his pockets, sir?' said Hartley, turning to the dramatist, and Lowe shook his head.

'Nothing,' he replied.

The superintendent frowned.

'I wonder who the fellow is?' he muttered. 'The first thing we've got to do is to establish his identity.'

He scratched his chin.

'We might as well get him out of that ditch, anyway,' he continued. 'Give me a hand, will you, Walsh?'

The constable, who had been standing by in silence, moved forward to the assistance of his superior. Between them they lifted the limp form out of the ditch and laid it down on the path at the side of the road. As soon as the body had been moved Lowe leaned forward and made a swift search of the place where it had lain.

'There's no sign of a weapon,' he remarked when he had finished, 'so the remote possibility that it was suicide can be ruled out.'

He walked over to the dead man and made a more careful examination than he had been able to do previously. He paid considerable attention to the hands and to the soles of the shoes. He found nothing that offered even the suggestion of a clue.

'I was hoping,' he said, straightening up, 'that there would be something that would tell us where this man had been shot.'

'Where?' said Hartley, rather puzzled.

Lowe nodded.

'Yes,' he answered. 'I don't think he was shot here. I think he was brought here after he was dead.'

'What makes you say that, sir?' asked the superintendent.

The dramatist pointed to the wound in the dead man's forehead.

'You can see that he's lost a considerable amount of blood,' he said. 'A great deal more than has run down his face and been soaked up by his collar. Apart from that, the exit wound made by the bullet is a fairly large one. There must have been even more blood from that, and yet if you look at the ditch where he was lying you'll find that there's not a trace of blood at all. That, in my opinion, proves that he was not put there until some time after he was dead.'

'I see what you mean, sir,' said Hartley.

He went over and peered down into the ditch.

'Yes, you're quite right, sir,' he continued, coming back, 'there isn't a trace of blood.'

'You don't want me any more, do you?' broke in Dr. Peters, a little impatiently. 'Because, if you don't, I'd like to get back. I had a pretty hard day yesterday, and to-day is going to be equally as bad. I'll let you have my preliminary report by nine o'clock.'

'If you wait a minute or two, Doctor,' said the superintendent, 'I'll come back with you. There's not much more we can do here.' He beckoned to the constable. 'You'll wait here, Walsh, with the body until the ambulance arrives,' he said.

'Yes, sir,' said Walsh, and the expression of his face showed that he did not relish the job that had been allotted to him.

'Were you thinking of going back to London, Mr. Lowe?' asked Hartley, and the dramatist after a momentary hesitation shook his head.

'No,' he replied. 'I think I shall stop in the neighbourhood for a few days; anyway, until after the inquest. Is there an inn or anything round here where my secretary and I could put up?'

'There's the Crossed Hands, in Stonehurst,' said the superintendent. 'It's a very quaint old place, but I don't know whether it will suit you.'

'If they can take us in it sounds admirable,' said Lowe.

'Oh, they'll be able to take you in all right,' answered Hartley. 'They don't get many visitors at Stonehurst. A man called Japper owns the place.'

'We'll knock up Mr. Japper,' said Lowe, 'and see what he can do for us.'

The superintendent issued his final instructions to the constable and, accompanied by Dr. Peters, followed Lowe and White across to the waiting cars.

'I'd like to see you in the morning, sir,' he said as Lowe climbed into his own car. 'You might give me a phone if you fix up at the Crossed Hands, and I'll come down.'

Lowe promised and the superintendent said good night.

Starting the engine, the dramatist backed the powerful car a few yards, swung the long radiator in the direction of the village, and pressed his foot on the accelerator pedal. As the machine gathered speed he heard the noisy chug-chug of the doctor's car as it drove off towards Hythe.

Constable Walsh watched the two cars receding in the distance and settled down to his lonely vigil, and as he waited for the arrival of the ambulance a man who had been watching and listening from the branch of a big elm that grew near the spot slipped noiselessly down from his place of concealment and moved cautiously off into the darkness of the night.

When he judged that he was out of earshot of the constable he began to run, and continued running until he arrived breathless at his destination.

5

Shots in the Night

The Crossed Hands was in darkness when Trevor Lowe and White arrived, but after their third knock a window was raised and a hoarse voice enquired what they wanted. Lowe explained, and the owner of the voice withdrew his head from the upper window, and after a delay of about five minutes, during which White became convinced that he had fallen asleep again, he appeared at the door.

'Come in,' he said huskily, holding up the oil-lamp he carried, so that they could see their way; and they crossed the threshold into a narrow passage, on either side of which were low archways that apparently led into the bars, for the dramatist caught a glimpse of counters with bottles and glasses.

The man who had admitted them opened a door at the side of the right-hand arch and ushered them into a comfortably furnished bar-parlour. The age of the place was apparent from the heavy oak beams which crossed the low ceiling and the discoloured stone work of the wall. Obviously very little had been done to the original building — at any rate this part of it — for there was no sign of even a suggestion of repairs or modern improvement. It was as it had been in the eighteenth century when the smugglers had met in the tap-room and made their plans to outwit the Preventive men.

The man who had let them in set the oil-lamp down on a table and eyed them a little suspiciously. He was a big fat fellow, with a large face that was nearly the hue of mahogany. His eyes were small and red-rimmed, and he was almost completely bald except for a thin wisp of reddish hair which stuck up in a tuft above his high forehead. Bloated was the word that leaped to Lowe's mind as he took in his appearance, and it was a very apt description.

'Are you Mr. Japper?' he asked, and the other nodded slowly.

'That's me,' he replied, and his voice was harsh and surly.

It gave Lowe the impression that he resented them. It may, of course, have been due to the fact that they had routed him out of his bed at this unearthly hour. But the proprietor of an inn ought to be prepared for these things. Whatever the reason was, Mr. Japper apparently suddenly realised his lack of cordiality, for he added hastily, and in a more conciliatory tone:

'What accommodation did you want, sir?'

'I want two rooms, if you've got them,' said Lowe, 'and if you can manage it, a meal of some sort.'

'I can manage the rooms all right,' replied the landlord, 'but the only thing I can get you, sir, in the way of a meal is bread and cheese and pickles. Will that be all right, sir?'

'That'll do excellently,' said the dramatist. 'Now, is there anywhere we can put the car?'

'There ain't a proper garage,' said Mr. Japper, 'but there's a barn round the back where it'd be all right.'

'Then perhaps you'll show my secretary where it is,' said Lowe.

The landlord hesitated for a moment, and Lowe was under the impression that he was rather reluctant to leave him alone. If he was he did not say so, but after a second's pause walked heavily to the door.

'If you come with me, sir,' he said, addressing Arnold White, 'I'll take you round.'

The secretary followed him out, and Lowe dropped into a chair and awaited their return. There was something about the landlord's manner that he did not like, but what it was he would have found it difficult to say. It wasn't his boorishness, it was something much more subtle than that. Those small red-rimmed unpleasant eyes had been watchful, and he had surprised in them once almost an expression of alarm. The man was afraid of something or other — what? He had reached no satisfactory conclusion by the time White and the landlord came back.

'Shall I show you the rooms now, sir?'

said Mr. Japper and Lowe nodded.

The landlord walked over to the lamp and picked it up.

'This way, sir,' he said, leading the way out into the passage, 'and be careful of them stairs; they're a bit narrow to those what's not used to them.'

The stairs were narrow and steep, almost like a ladder, but they reached the landing without mishap. Passing along a short corridor, Mr. Japper opened a door about half-way along and stood aside for Lowe to enter.

'This is one of the rooms, sir,' he said. 'The other's next door and a bit smaller.'

Lowe entered and looked round him. It was a low-ceilinged apartment, with panelled walls, and looked none too prepossessing in the flickering light of the landlord's oil-lamp. A large double-bed occupied most of the space, and facing the door was a latticed window with leaded panes. In one corner was a washstand and dressing-table combined, a cheap rickety affair that had nothing in common with the aged beauty of the old woodwork. This, with the bed and a couple of plain chairs, made up the entire furniture. The floor was polished and bare, except for one rug, rather worn and tattered, that occupied the centre of the room. It was by no means a luxurious apartment, but it was clean.

'This will do for me,' said Lowe. 'Let's have a look at the other room.'

The second room, slightly smaller and, except that the bed was a single one, was furnished almost exactly the same as the other.

'This will be all right for you, White, won't it?' asked the dramatist, looking at his secretary, and White nodded.

'Anything'll be all right for me,' he replied. 'I'm so tired I could sleep on a plank.'

'I suppose we can stay here for as long as we want to?' said Lowe, addressing the landlord.

'Oh, yes, sir,' replied Mr. Japper. 'We don't get many visitors nowadays. I'll be only too glad to have you.'

The tone of his voice, however, belied his words, and once again Lowe saw that momentary expression of fear flash into his little pig-like eyes.

They fixed on the terms, which were extraordinarily moderate, and returned once more to the bar-parlour.

'If you'll give me ten minutes, sir,' said the landlord, 'I'll go and get you your food. Would you like anything to drink with it?'

'I think a pint of ale would go down very nicely,' said Lowe, and the landlord withdrew.

'Not exactly the Ritz, is it?' remarked Arnold White as his heavy footsteps faded away in silence.

Lowe shrugged his shoulders.

'It's a fine old place,' he said, 'but it's been neglected. However, I think it'll suit us very well, and so long as the food is not too bad it will make a very good place to work from.' He took out his pipe and began to fill it from his pouch.

'You'd better go to town in the morning,' he went on, stuffing tobacco carefully into the capacious bowl. 'We shall want some things if we're going to stay.'

White nodded, suppressing a yawn.

'It's morning now,' he remarked. 'I wish that chap would hurry up with the food; I'm dying to go to bed.'

'I'm feeling a bit tired myself,' confessed Lowe.

'I wonder if that fellow in the ditch — ' began White, and stopped as the dramatist held up his hand with a warning gesture.

'Don't discuss things here,' he said in a low voice, and jerked his head towards the door. 'You don't know how far your voice carries and I don't want the landlord to hear too much.'

'Right you are,' said White, taking the hint, and began talking about nothing in particular until Mr. Japper appeared with a laden tray.

They were both hungry and welcomed the meal. The cheese was good and, embellished with pickled onions and washed down with light ale, formed an excellent repast. When they had finished Lowe rose and brushed the crumbs from his waistcoat.

'Now I think the next thing is bed,' he remarked, and almost as though he had heard, the stout landlord came in with two lighted candles.

'Have you had everything you require, sir?' he asked, glancing from one to the other.

'Yes, thank you,' said the dramatist.

'Then I'll say good night, sir,' replied Mr. Japper. 'What time would you like to be called?'

Lowe considered.

'Nine o'clock will do,' he said. 'And we'll have breakfast at half-past.'

'Thank you, sir,' said Mr. Japper. 'Good night to you both.'

They wished him good night and he withdrew.

Waiting until his heavy footsteps had ascended the stairs and they heard the closing of his door, they picked up the candle and followed. In the gloomy corridor they parted for the night — or rather for what remained of darkness — and retired to their respective rooms. Lowe undressed immediately and got into bed. To his surprise it was a great deal more comfortable than it looked. The mattress was well sprung and the overlay of feathers embraced his tired limbs with a degree of comfort that should have sent him to sleep at once. Perhaps it was due to this very fact that he remained wakeful. He was unused to a feather bed. He did not consider it healthy and preferred a harder mattress. Whatever it was, he was a long time getting to sleep, and lay staring at the darkness above him, his thoughts going over the events of the evening. Presently, however, he began to feel drowsy, and he was almost on the point of falling into a doze when he became dimly conscious of a sound in the house below. Only half-awake, he wondered vaguely what it could be, and decided that somebody was talking. The low muttered rumble of voices came plainly to his ears, and then as sleep descended on him suddenly all sounds were blotted out . . .

What it was that woke him he never knew, but he found himself sitting up in bed and staring at the oblong square that marked the position of the window. The dawn was breaking, and in the grey light he saw that one of the latticed panes was open, and half leaning through, shadowy and indistinct in that misty light, was the figure of a man. Even as Lowe looked the intruder raised one hand, and instinctively the dramatist threw himself sideways out of the bed.

Plop! There was a muffled sound and something struck the bed-rail close to where his head had been with a sharp tinkling sound.

Plop! Plop!

The man at the window fired again twice, and this time the bullets buried themselves in the pillow. Lowe was on his feet now, and as he made a rush for the window his foot caught against the leg of the bed and he fell sprawling. The crash he made must have frightened the night-marauder, for when he succeeded in scrambling to his feet the window was empty and nothing but the dawn light shining through!

6

Lowe Wonders

Trevor Lowe hurried over to the window and leaned out. It overlooked the back garden of the Crossed Hands, and beyond this was a vista of meadows and ploughed fields. In the grey haze of the coming day it was difficult to see very clearly, but the dramatist thought that there was a movement in the shadow of a tall hedge. Narrowing his eyes so as to get a better focus, he found that he was not mistaken. A crouching figure was hurrying away, and even as he looked it disappeared round a clump of laurel bushes.

It was useless attempting to follow. By the time he had put on some clothes and gone downstairs the shooter would have had ample opportunity for getting well away. He turned his attention to the wall of the house, to see how the intruder had managed to get to the window, and discovered that it had been simple enough. A ladder was reared up beside the casement, the top reaching a foot above the sill. Lowe withdrew his head, and going back to the bed, lighted the candle that stood on the little table by the head. He was in the act of blowing out the match when he heard a movement outside the door, and stood rigid. There came a gentle tap, and then White's voice called softly:

'Hullo! Mr. Lowe! Are you all right?'

Lowe went quickly over to the door and, unlocking it, pulled it open.

'Come in,' he said briefly; and as the secretary entered he shut and relocked the door behind him.

White, hastily attired in shirt and trousers, his eyes still heavy with sleep, looked about.

'What happened?' he asked. 'I heard a crash of some kind that woke me up.'

'You heard me fall down,' answered Lowe, and picking up the candle he went over to the head of the bed.

On the iron rail was a bright elongated mark, and in the pillow below, at a distance of only a few inches apart, were two neat brown holes. Arnold White at Lowe's elbow eyed these with wonder.

'What are they?' he asked.

'They're bullet holes,' replied the dramatist grimly, 'and it's very lucky for me that they are in the pillow and not in my head!'

The secretary's eyes widened.

'Bullet holes!' he exclaimed. 'How in the world did they get there?'

'They got there,' said Lowe, 'from the barrel of a silenced pistol that was fired from the window.'

While he took off the pillow-slip and cut into the striped tick beneath with his pocket-knife, he explained what had happened.

'Good God!' gasped White. 'Do you mean it was a deliberate attempt to kill you?'

'I do,' said his employer. 'That is exactly what it was.'

He searched in the feathers that his knife had laid bare and picked out two small blobs of lead, which he held out in the palm of his hand.

'Here are two of the bullets,' he

remarked. 'There's another one somewhere which struck the bed-rail and ricochetted. We may as well look for it.'

They found it over by the fireplace, flattened out of all semblance to its original shape.

'We'll keep these,' remarked Lowe, putting them into the pocket of his waistcoat that hung over a chair. 'They may prove to be a valuable clue if we can ever lay our hands on the pistol that fired them.'

All trace of sleep had vanished by now from White's eyes, and he frowned.

'I wonder who the fellow could have been?' he muttered. 'I suppose you weren't able to see him sufficiently to recognise him again?'

Lowe shook his head.

'I haven't the faintest idea what he was like,' he answered. 'I think — but I couldn't be sure — he was wearing a mask of some sort.'

He sat down on the edge of the bed and began to fill his pipe.

'One thing is certain,' he continued, 'whatever is at the bottom of all this, we're up against a particularly dangerous crowd. They strongly resent any interference with their business, whatever it is.'

White nodded.

'And they work pretty fast,' he grunted. 'I wonder how they knew that you'd put up at this place?'

'That wouldn't be very difficult,' said Lowe, slowly puffing at his newly lighted pipe. 'I've no doubt that somebody was watching us when we turned up to keep the appointment with the man who was killed, and that we were either followed here or I was overheard when I spoke to Hartley asking him about some place where we could stay. To-night's episode, however, has settled one point. Whatever it is that is going on, we're in the thick of it. It's centralised in this neighbourhood.

'I'd like to know what it is,' said Arnold White.

'So would I,' agreed the dramatist. 'And I'm going to know before I've finished. But we shall have to move very cautiously. I'm very anxious to know what happened to those Scotland Yard men, but I don't want to find out by sharing the same fate.'

'Do you think they have been killed?' asked White gravely.

'I should be very much surprised to find that they're still alive,' replied Lowe. 'Somehow or other they stumbled on this secret which is being so closely kept and paid the penalty. At least that is how I feel. Of course, it's only a theory at present, and there's very little data to work on, but what little there is points strongly to that supposition.'

They neither of them felt inclined to go back to bed, and presently, when the warm rays of the morning sun began to light the sky and sundry movements from outside told them that people were beginning to stir in preparation for the coming day, they washed and dressed and went downstairs. In the passage below they came across Mr. Japper, looking even more repellent if possible in daylight than he had done in the dim and more kindly light of the oil-lamp.

He was obviously surprised at seeing them about so early, and not a little suspicious.

'Thought you weren't getting up till

nine,' he said with a return to his original surliness of the night before. 'What's the matter? Weren't the beds comfortable?'

'The beds were very comfortable,' said Lowe, watching the man steadily. 'But it is not easy to sleep soundly when people come to your window in the middle of the night and entertain you with pistol practice.'

The flabby face of the landlord went a shade paler and his jaw dropped.

'What yer mean? Pistol practice?' he jerked.

His surprise was very well done, but not quite well enough. The expression of his eyes gave him away, and Lowe was convinced that he knew quite well what had been meant by pistol practice.

'Somebody climbed a ladder to my window,' he replied evenly, 'and shot at me during the early hours of the morning. If he had not made some slight sound which caused me to wake up and so defeat his object I shouldn't be talking to you now.'

'Nonsense!' declared Mr. Japper. 'You've had a nightmare, that's what you've had.

On account of that food you 'ad just before goin' to bed.'

'No amount of nightmare will account for these,' retorted the dramatist, and taking the three bullets from his pocket he showed them to the startled landlord.

Mr. Japper's apparent surprise turned to a look of horror.

'Where'd yer get those?' he said hoarsely.

'Two of them out of your pillow,' answered Lowe, 'and the third where it had fallen by the fireplace. And apart from these, if you take the trouble to go outside you'll find the ladder.'

'Well, I don't understand it, sir,' declared Mr. Japper, and his surliness had been replaced by a demeanour that was almost servile. 'I don't understand it at all.'

'I don't suppose you do,' said Lowe, 'but it's very peculiar all the same. Somebody knew I was staying here, and what is more, knew the room I was sleeping in.'

Mr. Japper rubbed his left hand up and down his thick, hairy right fore-arm.

Obviously he was trying to think of something to say. What he did say eventually sounded a little foolish.

'Very funny, ain't it?' he remarked.

'I have experienced better jokes!' said Lowe dryly. 'It didn't strike me as being in the least humorous!'

'I didn't mean it like that, sir,' said Mr. Japper hastily. 'What I meant was that it was — well, that it was queer.'

'Very queer,' said Lowe.

'Perhaps,' suggested the landlord, 'perhaps you'd rather not stay here now, sir, after — '

'Oh, I shan't alter my arrangements,' broke in the dramatist. 'Lightning seldom strikes twice in the same place, you know.'

'That's very good of you, sir,' said the landlord, but there was a tinge of disappointment in his voice, all the same. 'Would you like your breakfast now, sir?'

'As soon as you can manage it,' said Lowe, and then, as Mr. Japper was turning away, 'Can I have a look at your back garden?'

'Yes, if you wish, sir,' answered the man. 'That way, sir — through the door at the end of the passage.'

Lowe strolled towards the door he had indicated, and passing through he and White found themselves in the garden.

It was rather neglected, and almost the first thing the dramatist noticed was that the ladder had been removed. It was no longer reared against the wall by the window of the room he had occupied, but lying beside a shed that looked like a tool-house.

'I wonder who did that,' he said, pointing it out to his secretary. 'I'll bet it was Japper.'

'He never said anything when you mentioned it,' said White.

'There were a lot of things he didn't say,' replied his employer. 'I'm rather suspicious of that fellow.'

White raised his eyebrows.

'You don't think he was the man who tried to kill you, do you?' he asked.

Lowe shook his head.

'I know he wasn't,' he answered. 'The man who fired those shots was a much smaller fellow altogether, only half Japper's size. But I think Japper knows all about it. He wasn't really surprised, although he pretended to be.'

'Then you think he's mixed up in the other business?' said White.

'I think he knows about it,' said Lowe; 'and that's as far as I'm prepared to go at the moment. Let's see if we can find any trace of my early morning visitor.'

He walked over and examined the ground underneath the window of his room. The rain had rendered it soft, and there were several footprints. Among them he saw the mark of a large square-toed shoe, and followed it over to where the ladder rested by the shed.

'H'm!' he muttered. 'There's no doubt it was Japper who moved the ladder. That's his footprint right enough, and this' — he bent down and touched another and smaller impression beside the large print — 'this I should say is the print of the man who fetched it and put it up against the window.'

He tried to follow the tracks of the man after he had come down the ladder, and succeeded as far as the bushes where he had vanished. But after that point they emerged into a lane, and he lost them.

Coming back to the inn, they found breakfast awaiting them in the bar-parlour. It was served by a girl whom they had not seen before; a small wizened-faced girl with large, rather frightened eyes, whom they discovered was Japper's daughter. Lowe tried to engage her in conversation, but only succeeded in getting monosyllabic replies and gave up the attempt.

'That girl is frightened to death of something,' said Arnold White when she had gone out of the room to fetch a further supply of toast.

'Of her father, probably,' answered his employer. 'He's of the bullying type that would take a delight in exercising his authority on someone who was weaker than himself.'

After breakfast, while Arnold White went to prepare for his journey to town, he smoked and thought, and at ten o'clock, when his secretary had driven off, he enquired the way to the nearest telephone and set off along the High Street to the post office which housed it.

Superintendent Hartley answered his call and promised to come along and see him at lunch time.

'There's no further news at present, sir,' he said, in answer to Lowe's enquiry. 'The post mortem is being attended to this afternoon, and we're arranging for the inquest to be held the day after to-morrow.'

'You haven't succeeded in identifying the man yet, I suppose?' asked Lowe.

'No, sir,' replied Hartley, 'but I've had his description circulated, and we've taken prints of his fingers and sent them up to the Yard. I thought he looked as though he had passed through our hands at some time or another.'

'Criminal type, eh?' agreed Lowe. 'I thought that, too.'

He arranged to meet Hartley at the Crossed Hands and came out of the post office. The people he passed as he strolled back to the inn eyed him curiously and, he thought, resentfully. Obviously strangers were looked upon with suspicion and not welcomed in Stonehurst.

The news of the murder had spread

like an epidemic of influenza throughout the village, for he saw little groups of people standing at the doors of the cottages and at the entrances to the tiny shops and caught part of their conversation as he went past.

This was all very natural, and yet there was something he could not quite understand. It was a subtle something to which he found it impossible to give a name. An atmosphere that hung like a miasma over the entire place.

He puzzled over it for a long time, and was still puzzling when he got back to the inn.

It was just before Superintendent Hartley arrived that it suddenly came to him what this atmosphere was that he felt so strongly. Fear, that was it. Outwardly the village was like any other English village, peaceful, serene and beautiful, but underneath it was seething with cross-currents. Deep down in the depths was something of which he had only caught the vaguest glimpse. A horrible, beastly something that filled the pure air with the stench of corruption and spread forth that atmosphere of terror which brooded over the whole place.

He smiled to himself as he heard the voice of Hartley inquiring for him.

Was he allowing his imagination to run away with him, or was there really something at Stonehurst that was eating at the heart of that rural loveliness and making of it a village of terror?

7

McWraith Has an Idea

Jim Winslow came down to breakfast early — much earlier indeed than he had intended when he had gone to bed. But after the thing he had seen in the darkness of the night, he had found sleep difficult, and at last, after tossing restlessly about until the dawn broke, he had decided to get up. In the full light of the day he could scarcely bring himself to believe that the sight of the man stretched on the hospital ambulance had been real. But there by the window was the butt of the cigarette he had been smoking and the mark where it had burned into the wood of the floor, to testify that it had not been a figment of his imagination. He had really seen that thing being wheeled round the base of the Tower.

He felt annoyed with himself now that he had not gone out then and there and investigated the thing more closely. But almost directly after he had seen it it had come on to rain, and he had decided that paddling about in the rain was not any too inviting. Apart from which, he had for the moment believed that his eyes were playing tricks with him. By the time he had hesitated between going and stopping where he was he came to the conclusion that it was too late to do anything except go back to bed, and this he did, and spent the remainder of the night in restless wakefulness.

North was already up when he came down, and greeted him with an air of surprise.

'You are up early, sir,' he said.

'I didn't sleep very well,' answered Jim truthfully enough.

'I'm sorry to hear that, sir,' said North with concern. 'Did anything disturb you during the night?'

Jim was on the point of telling him what had disturbed him and then thought better of it.

'No, nothing,' he answered. 'It was the strange bed, I expect.'

While he waited for his breakfast he strolled out into the garden and made his way round to the foot of the Tower. There was a narrow path here which curved round the side of the house and intersected the drive about half-way down its length. It was along this path that he had seen the ambulance with its grim burden being pushed on the previous night, and as he reached it he looked down, hoping that he might find some confirmation of the sight he had seen. His hope was realised, for on the wet ground were the marks of wheels.

They came from a door in the Tower, and led in the direction of the drive. Jim followed the tracks, frowning, and found that at the place where the small path entered the drive the wheel marks stopped. Close by, however, were heavier depressions — the tracks of a car with almost new tyres that had stood for some time. Jim pursed his lips and gazed thoughtfully down at these signs on the wet ground. What had taken place at Greytower during the night? Something that was certainly very queer indeed if the evidence of his own eyesight and this further evidence was to be relied on. Somebody had brought out the wheeled ambulance from the lower room of the Tower and pushed it along the narrow path to the drive where a car had been waiting. So much was fairly plain. Presumably the man — alive or dead — whom Jim had seen on the ambulance had been transferred to the car, but why and by whom?

He walked back along the little path to the base of the Tower and tried the door. It was locked. The only person so far as Jim could see who could have been using the ambulance during the night was North. Beyond Ian McWraith and himself he was the only man in Greytower. But who was the other man? The man who had been lying so ominously still on the ambulance? Jim gave it up. There was something going on that appeared to him to be very sinister. The atmosphere of the place, that dreadful cry that had startled them almost immediately after their arrival, and the sight he had witnessed from his window were all part and parcel of something that was very queer indeed.

He made his way back to the house and found Mrs. North engaged in laying the table for breakfast. She greeted him quietly and respectfully, but there was something about her that had been absent on the previous night. Then she had been an emotionless automaton; now, in spite of her self-control, she was seething with an inward excitement. It was visible in the tightness of her lips and the brightness of her black eyes; in the slight but unmistakable trembling of her hands as she set out the knives and forks and spoons.

Jim went upstairs to wake up Ian McWraith, bewildered and distinctly uncomfortable, and Ian took some waking. He was fast asleep on his back and breathing heavily when Jim went in, and he took no notice when his name was shouted.

It was not until Jim took him by the shoulders and shook him violently that he showed any signs at all of returning consciousness. And then he groaned, opened his eyes, and stared blearily up into his friend's face with dawning comprehension.

'Wake up, you lazy beggar!' said Jim. 'Breakfast is nearly ready.'

McWraith grunted again, rubbed his eyes with the back of a huge hand, and laboriously hoisted himself to a sitting position.

'By Jove!' he gasped, blinking owlishly. 'I say, I didn't get tight or anything last night, did I?'

'Tight? No, why?' demanded Jim.

'I feel putrid!' grumbled McWraith. 'My mouth's like the bottom of a bird-cage and there's a steam engine at work inside my head.'

'Well, you only had one small whisky,' said Jim. 'You must have eaten something that disagreed with you.'

'I ate the same as you did,' answered McWraith getting gingerly out of bed and pouring himself out a glass of water. 'I suppose you feel all right?'

'I feel fine!' answered Jim truthfully. 'Well, I don't know what can be the matter with you, Ian, unless it's liver.'

'It must have come on very suddenly, if

that's what it is,' grunted his friend, emptying his glass in one gulp and filling it again. 'I've never felt like this before, except after a thick night.'

'It isn't that this time,' said Jim, and then he stopped suddenly and a queer expression came into his eyes.

'What's up?' demanded his friend, setting down his half-empty glass. 'Why the dopy expression?'

'I was just wondering,' said Jim slowly, 'if it was that whisky you had.'

McWraith stared at him.

'Don't be feeble,' he said scornfully. 'It'd take more than one small whisky to upset me.'

'Yes, if it was pure whisky,' retorted Jim. 'But supposing it wasn't pure? Supposing something had been put in it — ?'

'What the dickens are you getting at?' said McWraith seriously. 'Do you mean that it may have been drugged?'

'That's exactly what I do mean,' replied Jim, and then as the other snorted: 'No, I'm not fooling. Something very queer was happening here last night.'

He told McWraith what he had seen

from the window of his room and also what he had discovered that morning.

'God God!' exclaimed McWraith when he had finished. 'We seem to have dropped down right in the middle of a shilling shocker. You think that North drugged that whisky so that we shouldn't know what was happening during the night?'

Jim nodded.

'North or somebody,' he said. 'I've no doubt he thought that we should both have a night-cap and be quite safe until the morning.'

'And he probably still thinks so,' said McWraith. 'You had some soda, didn't you? They would have found two dirty glasses.'

He glanced at his reflection in the mirror over the dressing-table.

'I think you'd better keep quiet for the moment regarding what you saw, Jim. If you're right about this doping — and from the way I'm feeling at the moment I should think you were — North and the people with him — if any — are still under the impression that neither of us was in a fit condition to see anything — '

'North doesn't think that about me,' interrupted Jim. 'He seemed surprised that I was up so early, and I told him that I hadn't slept very well.'

'That's rather a pity,' growled McWraith, 'but still, you didn't tell him that you'd seen anything, did you?'

Jim shook his head.

'Well, that's all right, we'll let him remain under the impression that you didn't.' He grabbed a sponge-bag and a towel. 'I'm going to see if a bath will make me feel more like a human being, and then we'll discuss the matter still further. I feel that life is going to be very interesting round here.'

McWraith made his way to the bathroom and Jim went downstairs again. In the hall he found North hovering about with a can of hot water.

'Have you called Mr. McWraith, sir?' said the butler. 'I was just going to take him up his shaving water.'

'He's in the bathroom at the moment,' said Jim. 'Take the water up to him there, will you?'

'Yes, sir.' The butler turned towards the staircase, paused and looked back. 'By the way, sir, which will you have for breakfast, sir — tea or coffee?'

'Coffee, I think,' answered Jim, and the butler nodded and went up the big staircase.

McWraith, when he came down shaved and dressed, announced that he was feeling better; and when they had breakfasted suggested a walk.

'I'd like to see this village of yours,' he said. 'We didn't get much chance of seeing it last night, and, besides, it will be a new experience to walk through a village with the man who owns it.'

Jim was rather anxious to have a look at his property himself, and after arranging with North for luncheon at one he and McWraith left Greytower and set off to survey the land.

The morning was warm and bright and the air was full of the indescribable smell of earth after rain, which made McWraith sniff appreciatively.

'Don't know why anyone wants to live in crowded cities when they can get this sort of thing and pay less for it,' he remarked as they turned out of the drive and began to walk along the road that would bring them to the beginning of the village. 'This air is like a draught of wine, and much more healthy.'

'I always did like the country,' said Jim, 'and I think most people do. You've got to remember, though, Ian, that it's not easy for people who've got jobs in offices to live far away from them.'

'No, but I was thinking about the people who don't have to go regularly to work,' said his friend; 'and there are more of those than you'd think who prefer to be cooped up in a town. I suppose really it's a question of temperament.'

He lit a cigarette and tossed the match into a hedge.

'Now then, let's talk about last night,' he said. 'We're pretty safe here in not being overheard. Tell me again exactly what you saw.'

Jim told him.

'And this fellow on the ambulance,' questioned McWraith, 'would you know him again if you saw him?'

'Yes, I think so,' said Jim. 'The moon was shining pretty clearly and I got a good sight of his face. Yes, I'm sure I should know him again.'

'Do you think he was dead?' asked McWraith, and Jim hesitated before he replied.

'If he wasn't he was very ill,' he answered at length.

'He wasn't bound or anything?' said McWraith thoughtfully.

'That I couldn't say,' replied Jim. 'I didn't see closely enough.'

'H'm!' grunted the huge Scotsman. 'Well, the whole thing's most mysterious and interesting. I'll bet that butler of yours is at the bottom of it. A more unpleasant fellow I've never seen, and have you noticed that we haven't seen a sign of the dog he told us about last night?'

They had reached the end of a secondary road and were turning towards the village, when Jim, in the act of replying to McWraith's last remark, caught sight of a slim figure coming towards them and broke off.

Jill Heyford greeted them with a smile, and they both stopped.

'Good morning,' she said. 'Are you just looking round your property?'

'That's what we were going to do,' said Jim.

'You'll find it a very beautiful place,' said the girl. 'It's rather a pity, though, that this dreadful thing should have happened, isn't it?'

'What dreadful thing?' asked McWraith quickly.

She looked at him in surprise.

'Haven't you heard?' she said. 'A man was shot last night at the cross-roads just outside the village. Everybody says that it was — murder.'

She dropped her voice as she spoke the ominous word, and Jim and McWraith glanced sharply at each other.

'We've heard nothing about it,' said Jim. 'Who was it that was killed?'

'He was a stranger, I think,' said Jill. 'At least, nobody seems to know who he was in the village. The police may know.'

'And the murderer hasn't been caught?' said McWraith.

She shook her head.

'No, the whole thing appears to be a mystery,' she replied. 'The village is full of it this morning. Nobody can talk about anything else.'

'Well, a murder is an event anywhere,' remarked McWraith. 'And in a sleepy place like this, where I don't suppose anything much ever happens, I'm not surprised that it's caused an uproar.'

Except for the fact that he was watching her closely Jim might not have noticed the sudden change in the girl's expression. It was only momentary, but he noticed it, and made a mental note of what he had seen. It had coincided with McWraith's words — 'where I don't suppose anything much ever happens' — that sudden catching of the breath, the slight parting of the full red lips, as though she had been about to speak.

'We're not quite as sleepy here as you imagine,' she said, and the smile that accompanied her words was — or so Jim thought — rather forced. 'Quite a lot of things happen here, as you'll probably realise if you stay.'

There might have been nothing in her words. They were, after all, quite ordinary, but Jim thought that there was a hidden meaning behind them. That what she had meant was not quite what she had said.

She caught his eyes looking at her steadily, and suddenly became embarrassed.

'I — I must go,' she said quickly. 'I really ought not to have stopped gossiping. Good-bye!'

She gave a brief smile that embraced them both and hurried away up the road.

McWraith looked sideways at Jim as they continued on their way to the village.

'So there was a murder committed here last night,' he said softly. 'What do you think of that?'

'What should I think of it?' retorted Jim. 'The man was killed at the cross-roads — '

'Was he?' murmured McWraith, and his eyes narrowed. 'He was found at the cross-roads, but was he killed there?'

'Are you suggesting — ' began Jim; and McWraith stopped him with a nod.

'I'm suggesting,' he said seriously, 'that the man was killed at Greytower and that it was his dead body you saw being wheeled away on that ambulance during the night!'

8

Lowe Gathers Information

Superintendent Hartley set down his half-empty tankard, wiped his lips carefully with a large and spotless handkerchief, crossed his massive legs, and cleared his throat.

'Now, Mr. Lowe,' he said slowly, 'I should like you to give me a more detailed account of how you came to find the dead man if you will.'

Trevor Lowe considered for a moment before speaking. He had not as yet told the superintendent the reason that had brought him to the cross-roads on the previous night, but there was no object in keeping him in the dark. What he had seen of Hartley he liked. The man was by no means devoid of intelligence, and had none of the bumptious characteristics that are so often to be met with in a country police official.

He was the sort of man who would probably be of great help in the task that lay before the dramatist. He knew the surrounding country like a book and the people who lived there. All things considered, therefore, Lowe felt that it would be a good move to take him into his confidence.

'I'll tell you everything I know,' he said, and, removing his pipe from his lips, proceeded to do so.

He spoke in a low voice so that it would not carry beyond the confines of the bar-parlour in which they sat, and Hartley listened with great attention and without interruption until he had finished.

'Well, Mr. Lowe,' he commented when the dramatist had concluded, 'what you say throws an entirely new light on the matter. You think the dead man was the same person who rang you up?'

'I think it's more than probable,' said Lowe. 'Don't you?'

Hartley nodded.

'I think it's pretty certain,' he replied, 'and I also think it's pretty certain that he was killed to prevent him passing on the information he had to you.'

'That's my opinion,' agreed the dramatist. 'The question is, what was it he knew?'

'Yes, that's the question, sir,' said Hartley. 'What did he know? And what did these other fellows find out that led to their disappearance?' He shook his head gently. 'It's a funny business, isn't it?'

'It's a very grim business, Hartley,' said Lowe gravely. 'There's something very sinister about it, and the solution lies close at hand. That attempt on me last night was local.'

The superintendent finished the remainder of his beer and pursed his lips.

'Yes, sir,' he said thoughtfully. 'I think you're right.'

Something in his voice made Lowe give more attention to his words than their surface meaning.

'You know something?' he said quickly.

Hartley reddened, and looked a trifle embarrassed.

'No, sir,' he answered hesitantly. 'I don't rightly know anything, but — Well there's something that has struck me for a long time as being — peculiar, if you understand what I mean.' He stopped and wriggled on his chair uncomfortably.

'What is that?' prompted the dramatist gently.

'It may have nothing to do with what we were talking about, sir.' He was very red now, and one of his hands straightened his coat and the fingers started picking nervously at a button.

'I expect you'll think it's all nonsense, but — well, there *is* something queer about Stonehurst, sir.'

'In what way?' asked Lowe as he stopped again.

'Nothing that you would call tangible,' replied the superintendent; 'but I've lived in these parts, man and boy, for forty-five years, and I've noticed things. It's as if there were a kind of blight on the place, Mr. Lowe.'

Trevor Lowe leaned forward. Hartley had put into different words exactly the sensation he himself had experienced during the short time he had been in Stonehurst.

'Do you mean this particular village, or the whole of the surrounding country?' he said.

'Only Stonehurst, sir,' answered Hartley

hastily. 'Hythe and Dymchurch and places like those are just the same as they used to be.'

'But Stonehurst, isn't, eh?' said Lowe. 'How has it changed?'

'Well, the people are different for one thing, sir,' said the superintendent. He was more at his ease now that he saw Lowe's obvious interest.

'All the old families have gone — they've been what you might call frozen out, sir.'

'Do you mean forced to leave?' asked the dramatist, and Hartley nodded.

'Yes, sir, in a way,' he answered. 'I'll give you an example. There was Mr. Drilland, who used to live at Hartshorn Farm. His family had owned it for ages, and he had the finest herd of Jerseys in the district, and used to send his milk into Hythe. Well, about three years ago there was an epidemic in the town, and it was traced to a germ in this milk. Mr. Drilland went broke and had to sell the farm.'

'That's hard luck,' said Lowe, 'but I don't see — '

'That's only one example, sir,' said Hartley earnestly. 'There was old Dr.

Westfield. He'd been in Stonehurst for nearly forty years and had a good practice among the residents. About two years ago there were several deaths among the children, and it was proved that he'd made a mistake in mixing his medicines. Of course, he had to leave, and Dr. Grendon who's here now bought his practice. Then there was Formby, who had this place before Japper. His case was a bit more serious; he was found one morning with his head in the gas oven in the kitchen. There was no reason why he should have killed himself, but he did it.

'Some sort of disaster overtook all the old people who used to live here, sir, and I've thought for a long time that it was queer.'

'It certainly is queer,' agreed Lowe, frowning. 'Did all this happen within a given time?'

Hartley nodded.

'Yes, sir; within the last two or three years,' he said. 'The last bit of hard luck the village had was the death of old Mr. Winslow a few weeks ago. He owned the whole place.'

'Owned the whole place?' repeated the dramatist. 'Do you mean land and everything?'

Again Hartley nodded.

'Yes, sir.' He proceeded to tell Lowe the story.

'That's very interesting,' said Lowe, when he had finished. 'So Stonehurst is one of those privately-owned villages, is it? I've heard there are still a few left in England. Who owns it now?'

'Mr. Winslow's nephew, sir,' replied Hartley. 'He arrived yesterday, I believe.'

'You appear to know quite a lot about the place, although you live at Hythe?' said Lowe, and the superintendent smiled.

'Hythe's not so very far away, sir,' he answered, 'and I've got an old aunt who lives just at the bottom of the High Street. I come over to see her once a week, and she's a rare one to gossip.'

'I see,' said Lowe. 'Now tell me something about the people who have taken the places of those who were frozen out, as you put it.'

'There's Lady Thurley of Wood Dene,

what used to belong to the Taplows,' said the superintendent, ticking each name off on his large fingers. 'Her niece lives with her. And there's Mr. and Mrs. Gordon-Watts of the White House, and Mr. Lucia, who's just moved into the Martins' old cottage. He's a Frenchman, and I don't know anything about him. There's Dr. Grendon, who I told you about, and Mr. Toogood, who's got Hartshorn. Mr. Linney, who lives at the Lodge, and Mr. Netherton at the Bungalow. That's about all, I think, sir.'

'And none of these are local people?' asked Lowe. 'I mean they are all new inhabitants?'

'Yes, sir, all of them,' answered Hartley. 'There are a few of the old residents left, but they are mostly small farmers and farm labourers.'

'H'm!' Lowe rubbed his chin gently. 'I saw a lot of people in the village this morning that you'd hardly call villagers. Who are they?'

'I expect they're the servants of the persons I have mentioned,' answered the superintendent. 'They brought most of them with them.'

'And these extraordinary changes took place three years ago, you say?' murmured the dramatist.

'Roughly, sir,' answered Hartley. 'It started three years ago and it's been going on ever since.'

'It's queer' — Lowe pinched his lower lip — 'very queer. In three years Stonehurst seems to have suffered an invasion of strangers. I wonder why?'

The superintendent shrugged his broad shoulders.

'There may be nothing in it, sir,' he said. 'I don't want you to be influenced by anything I may think — '

'What *do* you think?' broke in Trevor Lowe quickly.

'Well, Mr. Lowe, I don't rightly know,' confessed Hartley, scratching his head, 'but it's always seemed funny to me. And somehow when you told me about these disappearances I sort of coupled the two things in my mind. I couldn't say why, though, if you asked me.'

'I'm very glad we've had this chat all the same,' said the dramatist. 'There's something definitely wrong going on, and whether what you've mentioned has anything to do with it or not, I'm going to find out what it is if I can.'

'I'd like to help, sir, in any way I can,' said Hartley eagerly.

'And I shall be very glad of your help,' answered Lowe. 'Between us we ought to be able to get to the bottom of the mystery.'

'There's one thing I'd like to suggest, sir,' said the superintendent a little diffidently, and hesitated.

'What's that?' asked the dramatist.

'Don't stop here, sir,' said Hartley seriously. 'If there is anything going on Japper may be in it, and it's dangerous.'

'I've considered that,' said Lowe, nodding.

'If you want a safe place to stay while you're carrying on your inquiries,' went on the superintendent, 'my old aunt's got a spare room in her cottage, and she could easily fix up an extra bed for your secretary.'

'I'll think about it, Hartley,' said Lowe. 'It seems a very good suggestion.'

'It's a *safe* suggestion, sir,' said Hartley meaningly, and stopped with a quick look round as there came a tap on the door and Mr. Japper entered.

'You're wanted, Super,' he said in his husky voice, his little eyes darting from one to the other. 'Mr. Winslow wants to speak to you.'

'Mr. Winslow?' For the moment Hartley was perplexed.

'Mr. James Winslow,' said the landlord. 'Old Winslow's nephew, the new owner of Stonehurst.'

9

At the Mortuary

Jim stopped dead in the middle of the road and stared at his friend with startled eyes.

'By Jove, Ian!' he exclaimed. 'I shouldn't be surprised if you aren't right.'

'I'm sure I'm right,' grunted McWraith grimly. 'It was the fellow who was found at the cross-roads whom you saw. It's hardly likely that there were two people killed last night.'

'I wouldn't like to swear that the man I saw was dead — ' began Jim, but McWraith interrupted him impatiently.

'Do you think he was drunk?' he asked sarcastically. 'I'll bet he was dead, and I'll bet that he was killed when we heard that scream.'

Jim shivered.

'If you're right, it's horrible!' he muttered; 'because you realise that North must have killed him himself, or been aware who did?'

'I shouldn't be surprised if he killed the man himself,' said McWraith coolly. 'That man would be capable of anything.'

'Well, I appear to have come into a pretty exciting inheritance,' said Jim. 'What do you think we ought to do, Ian?'

'I think we ought to try and get a look at the dead man,' answered the friend, 'and see if you can identify him as the man you saw on the ambulance.'

'That means informing the police,' said Jim.

'I'm afraid it does,' answered McWraith. 'I'm sorry about that, because I was looking forward to working this thing out on our own and keeping whatever excitement was going to ourselves. But we can't very well do that now. A case of murder is a serious business.'

'Well, then, we'd better get on with it,' said Jim. 'I suppose there's a police station in the place.'

'Let's go and see,' said McWraith, and set off with such enormous strides that

Jim had all his work cut out to keep pace with him.

They saw nothing in the way of a police station in the High Street, and Jim suggested that they should inquire at the post office. This was also a small shop that appeared to sell everything from a reel of cotton to a side of bacon, and the old man who appeared from an inner room after McWraith had nearly banged the counter to pieces to attract his attention was able to supply them with the information they required.

'We ain't got no police station at Stonehurst,' he said in a wheezy whisper. ''Ythe is the nearest.'

'Have you got a telephone?' asked Jim.

The shopkeeper stabbed with a rheumaticky finger at a dark corner.

'Over there,' he said asthmatically. 'It'll be sixpence.'

Jim paid the exorbitant fee and went over to the ancient instrument. The old man behind the counter waited, obviously listening. It was some time before Jim could get through, but at last he succeeded and stated his business.

'You'll have to see Superintendent Hartley, sir,' said the gruff voice that answered him. 'He's on his way to Stonehurst now to call on a gentleman who is stayin' at the Crossed Hands. You'll be able to catch 'im there.'

'What time's he likely to get there?' asked Jim.

'In about an hour, sir, I should think,' was the reply, and Jim thanked the man and rang off.

As he turned away after hanging up the receiver the old shopkeeper leaned forward.

'Be you old Mr. Winslow's nevvy?' he inquired, and Jim nodded.

'Are you thinkin' of stayin' up at Greytower, sir?' asked the old man. 'Permanent like?'

'I don't know yet,' answered Jim. 'I haven't made up my mind, but I think it's very probable. It's very beautiful round here.'

The old shopkeeper nodded his bald head slowly.

'Aye, it is that,' he said, and then he looked quickly all round him with sharp nervous glances and leaned forward until his lips almost touched Jim's ear. 'But if you take my advice, sir, you won't stop.'

The amazement that Jim felt was expressed in his face as he stared at the old man.

'Why not?' he demanded.

'Stonehurst ain't lucky to strangers, sir,' said the shopkeeper solemnly 'Things 'appen to people what tries to come and live 'ere.'

'What kind of things?' said McWraith, who had been listening interestedly.

'Queer things, sir,' replied the shopkeeper. 'Look what 'appened to that fellow last night, an' 'e was a stranger. The village didn't want 'im.'

'Are you suggesting that if I stop here the same thing will happen to me?' said Jim.

'No, sir, p'raps not that,' answered the old man; 'p'raps nothing 'll 'appen to ye at all. It depends whether the village wants ye 'ere. If it does — well, you'll be all right. If it don't, somethin' will 'appen.'

'It seems as though Stonehurst is a nice

hospitable spot,' remarked McWraith, and the old man looked at him queerly.

'It's all right,' he said, 'if you leave it be.'

Apparently he decided that he was saying too much, for before either of them could put any further question he turned abruptly away with a muttered good morning and disappeared through the door at the back of the shop. Jim looked at McWraith, and McWraith shrugged his shoulders.

'Well, you've got a nice property,' he said as they came out into the High Street, and Jim grunted.

'What do you make of it?' he said, frowning.

'Do you mean the old gentleman's warning?' asked McWraith. 'I think a great deal of it was superstition, but I also think that there was a grain of something else more material.'

'Well, it's all confoundedly interesting, Ian,' said Jim, 'and I don't mind telling you that if I had ever thought of not living here I've seen and heard enough to make me change my mind. There's something peculiar about this place, and I'm jolly well going to find out what it is.'

'I'm with you,' agreed McWraith heartily, 'and I'll stay and back you up. What are we going to do until this superintendent fellow turns up?'

'Have a look round the village,' said Jim. 'I'm rather interested to see if there are any visible signs of this marked antipathy to strangers.'

They explored the High Street from end to end, watched furtively by little groups of people who were gossiping at their gates and on whom a sudden hush fell as they approached. This silence continued until they had passed, and then was replaced by an excited whispering that was like a high wind blowing through a forest of trees. Whatever it was that was wrong with Stonehurst, it certainly was not the village itself, for a more beautiful place Jim had never seen.

The half-timbered old cottages with their thatched roofs, picturesquely screened by the trees that surrounded them; the cobbled High Street, from which narrow lanes wound away to open fields and woods;

the old forge still in use at the bottom of the hill, and the little poky shops with their windows of thick green glass that distorted the goods behind until they bore no resemblance to what they really were; the square tower of Greytower that rose above the foliage like a watchful sentinel, and the complete absence of all the rush and bustle associated with modern life, combined to make the place a backwater of beauty and peace: the very incarnation of one of those woodcuts that may be found in very old books.

Jim and McWraith were enchanted with it, and the hour that they had set themselves to while away became nearly two before they realised it.

'By Jove!' exclaimed Jim suddenly as the cracked bell in the ancient church proclaimed that it was half past twelve. 'We'd better hurry back to the Crossed Hands or that superintendent fellow will have gone.'

They found a sprinkling of villagers in the bar when they entered, who stared at them curiously as Jim approached the counter and spoke to the stout man who was slowly sipping from a tankard.

'Has Superintendent Hartley arrived yet?' asked Jim. 'If he has, will you tell him that Mr. Winslow would like to speak to him?'

Mr. Japper lowered the tankard and regarded Jim with interest.

'The Super's here now, sir,' he said. 'Are you old Mr. Winslow's nephew?'

'I am,' said Jim.

'Pleased to see you, sir,' said the landlord, 'and I'd like to take this opportunity of hoping that you'll settle down at Greytower.'

Jim thanked him, and wiping his hand on his apron, Mr. Japper disappeared through a door at the back of the bar. He was gone for less than a minute, and when he returned it was by an archway that led into a passage.

'If you'll step this way, sir, I'll take you to the Super, sir.'

Jim went out into the passage, followed by McWraith, and the landlord conducted them to a door on the right.

Opening it, he ushered them into the room beyond, and Jim saw that it was occupied by two men. A large man who had 'policeman' written all over him and another of medium height whose pleasant humorous eyes were regarding him with a look of interest.

'You wanted to see me, sir?' asked the large man as Mr. Japper withdrew.

Jim nodded.

'Yes, if you're Superintendent Hartley,' he replied.

'That's me, sir,' said Hartley; 'this gentleman is Mr. Trevor Lowe.'

McWraith gave an exclamation.

'Are you the dramatist?' he asked.

'I've written several plays,' replied Lowe with a smile.

'I saw one of them three nights ago,' said McWraith. 'Jolly good, it was.'

'I'm glad you liked it,' murmured Lowe.

'What was it you wanted to see me about, Mr. Winslow?' asked the superintendent.

'I understand,' said Jim, 'that a man was found shot dead at the cross-roads outside the village last night. Is that correct?'

'Quite correct, sir,' nodded Hartley.

'Well, if it's possible, I should like to see the body,' Jim went on. 'I think I may be able to supply you with some useful information.'

'Does that mean that you think you know the man, sir?' said Hartley quickly.

'By name, no,' answered Jim, 'but I think I may have seen him before. The best thing I can do is to tell you all about it.'

Without preamble he began to give them an account of what he had seen from the window of his room on the previous night. Both Hartley and Lowe listened with great interest.

'I can't be sure that it was the same fellow, of course,' Jim concluded, 'but I'd know if I could see him.'

'That'll be easy, Mr. Winslow,' said the superintendent. 'I've got my little car here, and I can drive you over to Hythe now if it's convenient.'

'What do you say, Ian?' Jim looked at his friend, 'It'll mean postponing our lunch.'

'I say, carry on,' answered McWraith.

'What is a lunch more or less in the cause of justice?'

Superintendent Hartley looked doubtful.

'I'm afraid,' he said deprecatingly, 'that I can't take your friend, Mr. Winslow. My car's only a small one — '

McWraith grinned.

'That's all right,' he said. 'Don't you worry about me. You can carry on with the good work, and while you're gone I will make the acquaintance of the good ale of Stonehurst.'

'Sure you don't mind?' said Jim. 'We could go and get our own car if you like, and — '

'No, no,' boomed McWraith. 'You cut along and get it over while I try and see if I can find another sort of body — perhaps the beer down here has got some for a change!'

They left him to sample it and climbed into the superintendent's dilapidated car. Although its appearance suggested that it was only fit for the scrap-heap, they quickly discovered that this was deceiving, for it was capable of a good speed, and ate up the ten miles that lay between Stonehurst and Hythe in just over fifteen minutes.

Hartley drove straight to the mortuary, and presently Jim found himself bending over a low trestle-table on which lay a motionless figure covered by a sheet.

'Now, sir,' said Hartley, 'perhaps you'll just tell us if this is the man you saw.'

He pulled down the sheet, and Jim looked at the white face that was disclosed. For a second only he looked, and then he straightened up and turned to Lowe and the superintendent.

'That is the man,' he said briefly.

10

In the Tower Room

'Well, this fresh information seems to indicate that the man was killed at or in the vicinity of your house, Mr. Winslow,' said Trevor Lowe gravely, 'and that would also seem to implicate your butler.'

Jim nodded with knit brows.

'I've been thinking the same,' he admitted.

They were back again in the parlour of the Crossed Hands and had collected McWraith from the bar to join them.

'As I said before,' remarked that huge man, balancing himself precariously on the edge of the table, 'it wouldn't surprise me in the least to hear that North was the actual murderer. I'm sure the man's face would hang him if he ever appeared in the dock.'

'I took an instant dislike to him,' said Jim. 'There's something horribly shifty about the man.'

'H'm!' said Lowe thoughtfully. 'I should like to see this unpleasant person and also have a look at the Tower room, and that ambulance.'

'Come back to lunch,' suggested Jim; 'we're terribly late, but if it's spoiled I dare say Mrs. North will be able to rake up something eatable.'

'Thanks, I'd like to,' replied the dramatist.

'You'll come, too, Superintendent, won't you?' said Jim, turning to Hartley.

'Thank you, sir,' said the superintendent.

'Then, suppose we make a move.' Jim rose to his feet. 'I must say that I'm beginning to get hungry.'

'I've been hungry for a long time,' growled McWraith. 'There may be a lot wrong with Stonehurst, but you can take it from me that the beer's all right. It's given me a prodigious appetite.'

Lowe had a word with Mr. Japper, in case White should return during his absence, and then the little party set off for Greytower. Lowe and Jim walked on ahead, Hartley and McWraith bringing up the rear.

'If North has got anything to do with the business,' Jim remarked, 'it'll be interesting to see his face when I arrive with the superintendent.'

'It may be very instructive,' said Lowe. 'Tell me, what time was it when you heard that scream?'

Jim thought before he replied.

'I'm not quite sure,' he said at length, 'but it was somewhere between seven and eight — nearer eight, I should think.'

'That complicates matters a bit,' said Lowe musingly.

'Why?' asked Jim, a little puzzled.

'Because,' answered the other, 'we were assuming that scream you heard was the death cry of the man who was killed. But either it was nothing of the sort or the man I found in the ditch was not the same man who rang me up.' He rubbed his chin gently. 'My telephone call was at twenty minutes past ten,' he went on, 'and if he had been killed when you heard the scream he couldn't have phoned. And yet I'm pretty certain that the dead man was the man who made the appointment. It was the making of that appointment that brought about his death.'

'Then, who screamed?' demanded Jim.

'That's what I should like to know,' replied Lowe, drawing his brows into a frown. 'Who screamed?'

He was lost in thought until they turned into the drive, and then he roused himself and looked about him.

'I'd like to stop and have a look at this path you mentioned,' he said. 'The one on which you found the marks of the wheels.'

'It's farther up,' said Jim. 'I'll show you when we come to it.'

A little farther on he stopped at a break in the shrubbery that lined the drive.

'Here you are,' he said. 'The marks of the car are just there.'

The dramatist stared at the ground and then looked round at Jim.

'Where?' he asked quietly.

'There,' said Jim, coming over to him; 'just — ' He broke off; the tyre marks he had seen that morning were no longer there. 'But — but — ' he stammered, completely taken aback. 'They *were* there, Mr. Lowe.'

'I can see that something was there,' interrupted Lowe, 'but whatever it was has been carefully erased — with a stiff brush, I should think by the look of it.'

'What have you found, sir?' inquired the voice of Hartley. He and McWraith had been walking more slowly than Lowe and Jim, and had only just caught up with them.

The dramatist explained and the superintendent's lips formed themselves into a silent whistle.

'So someone has been removing traces, have they?' he murmured.

'It looks like it,' said Lowe. 'Let us see if they've done the same thing to the traces of the ambulance on the smaller path.'

He turned into the narrow opening between the bushes and, stooping, peered at the ground.

It was free from any sign of a wheel-track, but here, as in the drive, the marks of stiff bristles were plainly visible.

'Somebody has been extremely busy,' remarked Lowe, straightening up, 'covering up all traces.'

'And that somebody must have been my butler, North,' said Jim.

'It certainly looks extremely like it,' agreed the dramatist, 'or, at any rate, he must have known about it. I think I should like to follow this path round to the Tower and see if we can find anything there.'

Without waiting for Jim to reply he set off walking slowly along the narrow path, while the others followed him. The person who had destroyed the tracks made by the ambulance had been thorough, for although Lowe kept his eyes fixed on the gravel, there were no signs of any wheel-marks. They came out presently by the Tower, and Lowe gazed at the grim pile of masonry with interest.

'This looks as if it were very old,' he said. 'Much older than the rest of the house.'

'I believe it is,' answered Jim; 'it was originally a Martello tower, and the rest of the house was built on to it.'

Lowe nodded and examined the ground round the base of the Tower. But here, too, the broom had been busy, and there was nothing in the way of tracks. He tried the door, but it was locked.

'It was in the room behind this door that you saw the ambulance affair, wasn't it?' he asked, turning to Jim, and the latter nodded. 'I'd like to have a look inside,' he went on. 'Can you manage to get hold of the key?'

'I'll go and find North,' said Jim, and set off on his errand.

While they waited for his return Lowe took stock of the rest of the house. It was very solidly built; there was no modern building here, and it looked as though it could withstand a siege. The stone walls, with their covering of ivy, suggested a sense of strength and power. It required very little imagination to conjure up a drawbridge and a moat and guess at the portcullis that had probably at one time guarded the entrance.

Jim was gone some time, but when he returned he returned alone.

'I thought it was better in the circumstances not to let North know that you were here or what you were doing,' he said, 'so I managed to slip in and get the key without either he or his wife being aware of the fact.'

'Good man!' said Lowe, and took the heavy bunch from Jim's hand. 'I suppose you don't know which of these is the right one?'

Jim shook his head.

'I don't know anything about them,' he said, 'except that I noticed last night where North kept them, which was lucky.'

Lowe went over to the massive oak door which years of exposure to all kinds of weather had rendered black and iron-hard and tried several of the keys in the lock. At his fourth attempt he found one that fitted. It turned easily, and as he withdrew it he saw that the wards were slimy with oil.

'Your butler appears to take great care of the locks,' he said to Jim as he pushed the big door and entered the gloomy dungeon-like room beyond.

It was very difficult to see anything at first, for the single slit of a window allowed scarcely any daylight to filter through. But the dramatist had brought his torch with him, and its brilliant white light soon dispersed the darkness. So far as Jim could see the place was exactly as he and McWraith had seen it on the previous night. The packing-cases still stood against the wall, the broken chair was where it had been then, and by the iron bedstead stood the ambulance.

Lowe went over to it and carefully examined it. There was no doubt that it had been recently used. There was no dust on it, and the wheels, though they had been wiped, still showed traces of mud where the tyres fitted into the rims. Suddenly he bent forward and peered at a crack in the enamelled headrest fitted into the remainder of the contraption.

'There's something here,' he murmured, with narrowed eyes, and taking out his penknife, he opened it and inserted the point of the blade into the interstice.

When he withdrew it and looked at it in the light of his torch he drew in his breath with a sudden hiss.

'Look at that, Hartley,' he said, holding it up so that the superintendent could see it.

Hartley stared at the shining steel and saw that a small portion of it was dyed red — a red that glistened in the light of the torch.

'Good God, Mr. Lowe!' he breathed, 'it's blood!'

Trevor Lowe nodded grimly.

'Yes,' he answered, 'it's blood, and it's comparatively fresh!'

11

North is Frightened

Jim looked at the sinister stain on the penknife, and, in spite of himself, gave a little shiver.

'Although this trolley has been carefully cleaned,' said Lowe, laying his hand on the ambulance, 'the blood in this crack has been overlooked. Probably if the person who cleaned the thing had had more time he wouldn't have overlooked it. But it proves that the man you saw, Mr. Winslow, was wounded, and wounded in the head, for this is where his head would naturally rest.'

'And the man who was killed was shot through the head, sir,' said Hartley.

'Exactly.' Lowe nodded slowly. 'I don't think there can be much doubt that they were the same, in which case it seems more than likely he was shot here.'

He wiped the penknife on the arm of

the old chair and, folding it, put it back in his pocket.

'I think we'll have a look round,' he continued. 'There is a chance we may find the bullet that killed him.'

While Jim and McWraith looked on he and Hartley began a systematic search of the Tower room, but they found nothing.

'What about this, sir?' asked Hartley as he came upon the door under the winding stone staircase. 'Where does this lead to?'

Jim repeated what North had told them on the preceding night.

'I wonder if he was speaking the truth,' muttered Lowe, and going over he looked keenly at the iron barrier, running the light of his torch up and down the hinges and the jamb.

'I'm inclined to think he was lying,' he announced presently; 'unless I'm very much mistaken, this door has been opened recently.'

'Perhaps one of those keys you have will fit it,' suggested Jim, and Lowe tried them.

But none of them fitted.

'There must be another key somewhere,' said Lowe, 'and until we find it it's hopeless trying to do anything. Only a charge of dynamite would shift this door.'

He left it and came back to the centre of the stone chamber.

'I'd like to have a look over the rest of the Tower,' he said, 'though I don't suppose we shall find anything. Whatever there may be is behind that door, in spite of your butler's assertions that it has not been opened for years.'

Jim led the way up the stone staircase, and Lowe and the other followed. The dramatist searched each room thoroughly on the way up, but, as he had expected, there was nothing. They reached the battlemented top and Lowe admired the wonderful view of the rolling country to the sea. It was a clear day, and the lightship marking the sand-bar and the Dungeness lighthouse were plainly visible. Neither he nor Jim guessed as they looked at the finger of stone projecting from the sea, the sun glistening on the glass of the lantern, what a big part it was to play in the events that were to follow.

They returned to the ground floor, locked up the entrance to the Tower, and made their way round to the front of the house.

There was nobody about, but the table in the dining-room was laid for lunch. Jim suggested that they should help themselves to drinks which stood on a tray on the sideboard, and rang the bell. There was some delay before he got any answer, and then instead of North, as he had expected, Mrs. North tapped at the door and entered.

'I'm sorry, sir,' she apologised, 'but my husband is not very well. He's gone to lie down, sir. I hope you will excuse him.'

She looked rather ill at ease, and for the first time Jim noticed a trace of emotion in that usually expressionless face.

'I'm sorry to hear that, Mrs. North,' he said. 'What's the matter with him?'

'I don't believe it's anything serious, sir,' she said hastily. 'He's suffering from a bilious headache. Would you like luncheon now, sir?'

'Yes, please,' answered Jim. 'I'm sorry we're late, but we were detained on business.'

The woman's eyes flickered round the group.

'Will there be four of you?' she asked,

and Jim nodded.

'Yes, can you manage something?' he said.

'Oh, yes, sir,' she answered. 'I'll have it ready in a few minutes.'

She made her strange little half bow, half curtsy, and withdrew.

McWraith, who was pouring out whiskies and sodas, turned as the door closed behind her.

'I wonder if that's true — about North,' he said.

'I rather doubt it,' replied Lowe. 'If you want my opinion, he's found out that you have taken the keys, saw that we were here, and provided himself with an excuse to keep out of the way.'

'But what good would that do him?' asked Jim, taking the glass that McWraith handed him. 'He can't use the excuse of being ill permanently.'

'He may have some special object in wanting to keep out of the way to-day,' said Lowe. 'I think, however, we should be justified in insisting on seeing him after lunch. Don't you, Hartley?'

'I do, sir,' agreed Hartley with emphasis; 'there are quite a lot of questions I should like to put to him.'

Lowe smiled.

'I can think of one or two myself,' he said. 'Also I shall be very interested to see that dog of his which screamed last night.'

'I've seen no sign of a dog,' said Jim.

'I don't mind betting,' put in McWraith, 'that the dog only exists in North's imagination. He knew what it was that made that horrible row, and he had to account for it somehow. The dog was the first thing that came into his head.' He gulped down his drink and put the empty glass back on the tray. 'What do you think is at the bottom of all this?' he asked, looking from Lowe to Hartley.

The dramatist shrugged his shoulders.

'I haven't the least idea,' he replied candidly. 'I'm as much puzzled as anybody, but I'm hoping that we may strike something if we keep on long enough. Whatever it is, this murder is only part of it, and a very small part at that.'

He considered a moment, looking from McWraith to Jim and back again. Would he be justified in taking them entirely into his confidence. He was a great believer in first impressions, and the first impression of both these men was a good one. He decided to risk it.

'Stonehurst holds a secret far greater than the killing of this unknown man at the cross-roads,' he said. 'That was only an episode made necessary because he knew something which would have proved disastrous for somebody if he had been allowed to speak.'

Rapidly he related the gist of his interview with Shadgold, and Jim and McWraith listened enthralled.

'By Jove!' exclaimed the big Scotsman. 'This sounds jolly interesting. What do you think happened to these Scotland Yard men?'

'I'm very much afraid that they're dead,' answered Lowe gravely. 'In my opinion they, too, found out something connected with Stonehurst's closely guarded secret and were silenced.'

There was a moment's hushed silence, broken at last by Jim.

'What the dickens can be at the back of it all?' he said.

'That is what I'm trying to find out,'

declared Lowe. 'And whatever it is, I think your butler knows all about it.'

'Then we'll jolly well make him talk!' said McWraith.

'We'll try,' agreed the dramatist, 'but I doubt if it's going to be as easy as you think. There's somebody in the background directing operations who apparently sticks at nothing to ensure silence, and North — if he knows anything — will be aware of this. Fear is one of the strongest of human emotions to overcome.'

Before they could discuss the matter further Mrs. North came in with a dish of beautifully grilled and very succulent-looking chops, and since they were all ravenously hungry by this time, the subject of the mystery surrounding Stonehurst was stopped by tacit consent while they fortified themselves with this excellent food. A very good Stilton followed, and when the housekeeper had set coffee before them and Jim had handed round a box of cigars McWraith expressed the feelings of everybody in words.

'That's better,' he remarked with a sigh of content, settling his huge form back in his chair. 'I don't remember ever having felt so hungry.'

'I felt hungry, too,' said Hartley, carefully lighting a cigar. 'I must say, Mr. Winslow, that your housekeeper knows how to grill a chop.'

'I hope we shall be able to 'grill' Mr. North as well,' said Lowe, smiling. 'Suppose we have him in now?'

Jim rose and rang the bell.

'You'd better ask for him, Hartley,' said the dramatist. 'You're the only person here with official standing.'

Hartley nodded.

'All right, sir,' he said; 'you leave it to me.'

There came a preliminary tap at the door, and Mrs. North entered. She was crossing to the table, evidently under the impression that the bell had been a signal for her to clear away, when Jim stopped her.

'Mrs. North,' he said, 'Superintendent Hartley wishes to speak to you.'

The woman started, and her sombre face went a shade paler.

'Yes, sir?' She turned her large black

eyes towards the superintendent.

'I'm sorry to trouble you, Mrs. North,' said Hartley genially, 'but I should like to see your husband for a few minutes.'

The pallor underneath her olive skin increased, and she passed the tip of her tongue over dry lips before she replied:

'He's in bed, sir. Was it very important?'

'Yes,' answered the superintendent; 'but if you like, I can go up to his room — '

'There's no need to do that, sir,' she broke in quickly. 'I'll go and tell him, and ask him to come down.'

She went to the door with a sharp jerky movement, and when she had gone Lowe looked across at the superintendent.

'That woman's scared,' he said.

'I hope North isn't sufficiently scared to run away first,' said Hartley. 'Have you thought of that?'

'Yes, it did cross my mind,' answered the dramatist, 'but I don't think he'll go as far as that. He's sensible enough to realise that he could easily be caught, and flight would be as good as a confession of his guilt. I think now that he finds that he's got to he'll face it out.'

Ten minutes passed, and then there came a gentle tap at the door and the butler entered. Except for his collar and tie, he was fully dressed beneath a dressing-gown he wore. His narrow, ferret-like face was yellow, and his appearance suggested that there might have been some truth in Mrs. North's statement that he was suffering from a bilious attack.

'You wanted to speak to me, sir?' he asked deferentially, standing just inside the doorway.

'Yes.' Hartley cleared his throat. 'I want to ask you a few questions concerning the murder that took place outside the village last night.'

Lowe, watching intently, saw the butler's hands clench, but he gave no other sign that he was in the least perturbed.

'I've heard about it, of course, sir,' he said easily. 'The tradespeople were full of it this morning, but otherwise I'm afraid I know nothing about it.'

'You wouldn't, Gillman,' said Lowe

suddenly. 'Blackmail is more in your line, isn't it?'

North started violently and his head shot round towards the speaker.

'I don't know what you mean, sir,' he said, but his voice was high and shaky. 'My name is North — '

'Your name is Joseph Gillman,' snapped Trevor Lowe, 'and the last time I saw you was in the dock at the Old Bailey charged with blackmail!'

12

Through the Window

North's face changed from yellow to a dirty grey.

'I assure you you are making a mistake, sir,' he said, licking his lips. 'My name is not Gillman; it's North.'

'It may be now,' said Lowe, 'but it was Gillman then. That's seven years ago, if I remember rightly.'

'Are you sure of this, sir?' asked Superintendent Hartley.

'Quite sure,' replied Lowe with conviction. 'I never forget a face. I was spending some little time at the courts in order to get some technical details for one of my plays, and I remember seeing this man sentenced. But you can easily prove what I say. Take his fingerprints and send them up to the Yard.'

'There's no need to do that,' muttered North; 'you're quite right; I am Gillman.

But I'm running straight now, that's why I changed my name. I got sick of going crooked, sir; it doesn't pay in the long run, and after that last sentence I swore I'd go straight. I was lucky to get this job — '

'On forged references?' suggested Hartley.

The butler shook his head.

'No, sir,' he said, 'the old gentleman — old Mr. Winslow — knew all about me. He was kind enough to give me a job.'

'We've only got your word for that,' grunted the superintendent.

'It's the truth, sir,' said North. 'Honest, it is.'

'If Mr. Winslow knew about you, why did you have to change your name?' asked Lowe.

The butler looked a little disconcerted.

'Well, sir,' he replied after a second's delay, 'other people might have recognised it, and it would have been rather awkward.'

'I've no doubt it would,' said Lowe dryly, and then suddenly: 'What made you ill? Did you catch a chill last night?'

'I didn't go out last night, sir,' said the butler quickly.

'Then who took out that ambulance that you keep in the Tower room?' asked Lowe sharply.

'No one, so far as I know,' said North. 'Was it taken out?'

'You know very well it was,' said the dramatist. 'It was taken out of the Tower room and wheeled round to the drive where somebody was waiting with a car.'

North's face showed the utmost surprise. Rather overdone, McWraith thought.

'I assure you I know nothing about it,' he protested. 'I was in bed and asleep at twelve, sir.'

'I never said anything about the time,' snapped Lowe, and North looked embarrassed.

He tried to rectify his blunder, and in doing so gave himself completely away.

'I — I thought' — he stammered — 'I was under the impression that the — the dead man wasn't found until after that time — ?'

He floundered helplessly and his voice trailed away to silence.

'I don't know why you should connect that fact with my remark concerning the ambulance,' said Trevor Lowe. 'I never mentioned anything about the dead man.' He paused to give the butler an opportunity of speaking, but North, his face grey and haggard, remained mute. 'Did you connect the two,' Lowe went on relentlessly, 'because you knew the ambulance had been used to transport the body of the man who was killed from the Tower room to the waiting car, which took it to the place where it was found?'

Still silence from the frightened man by the door.

'You did know,' said Lowe harshly. 'You may have gone to bed at twelve, but you got up again to assist at the killing of the man I found in the ditch at the cross-roads. He was killed here — at Greytower — in that locked room, the door of which you said had never been opened to your knowledge, but which I know was opened recently.'

North's lips moved, soundlessly at first, and then words came huskily, incoherently pouring themselves out in a stream of denial.

'I don't know anything about it,' he

cried huskily; 'I swear I don't. You're trying to fix something on me because I'm an old lag. I didn't kill the man and I don't know who did. That's the truth — whether you believe it or not; that's the truth and you can't put anything over on me!' His voice rose shrilly. 'I'm not in this business at all, I don't know anything.'

He was lying, and they knew that he was lying. There was no ring of truth in that outburst; only fear — fear for his own skin, and the dramatist decided to play on that fear.

'I don't believe you, Gillman,' he said sternly, 'and I'm pretty certain that the jury won't either.'

The butler's face changed from its yellowish grey to a dirty, unpleasant looking white.

'The jury?' he muttered. 'Why — what — '

'That's what it'll come to,' said Lowe. 'You surely realise that there is sufficient evidence to warrant Superintendent Hartley detaining you for the murder of this unknown man?' He glanced quickly at Hartley, and the superintendent picked up his cue.

'That's right,' he said gruffly; 'I shall have to ask you to come along with me to the station.'

North gave a little choking sound that was half a sigh and half a cough, and his small eyes shifted from face to face like a trapped stoat.

'I swear to you I had nothing to do with it — ' he began, his voice shaking with terror.

'You may not have actually shot the man yourself,' said Lowe, 'but you know who did, and therefore are an accessory, and in cases of murder an accessory is regarded as equally guilty.'

'I — I — ' North swallowed hard, as though he had difficulty in speaking. 'Look here, supposing I tell you all I know — that'd go in my favour, wouldn't it?'

Lowe's pulses quickened; this was what he had been playing for — hoping that the man's nerve would break.

'Yes,' he answered, 'you would certainly get off with a lighter sentence. Wouldn't he, Hartley?'

'Without a doubt, sir,' said the superintendent.

'Well, then, listen.' North glanced uneasily round the room, as though he expected some menacing figure to leap out on him from behind the furniture. 'I've only been doin' what I was forced to do.' He came two or three steps nearer to Lowe and Hartley. 'I couldn't help myself; there's a devil in Stonehurst and — '

Crash!

The glass of the window overlooking the garden shattered to fragments, and North staggered. His hands went up, clawing wildly at the air, his face contorted into a grotesque expression of horror and surprise, and then suddenly he collapsed, fell across a chair, slithered from there to the floor and lay still.

'Good God!' gasped the startled superintendent. 'What was that?'

Without answering, Lowe stepped over to the prostrate figure of the butler and bent down. A glance showed him that the man was dead, and the spreading stain on the breast of his dressing-gown was mute evidence of how death had come to him.

'That was a bullet,' he snapped. 'Somebody shot him through the window.'

'But — ' began Hartley, and found that he was speaking to empty air, for in two strides Lowe had reached the door, jerked it open and disappeared into the hall.

Rather shaky and white, Jim and McWraith followed him. The front door was open, and they could hear his hurried steps on the gravel outside. Presently they came up with him standing underneath the window through which the shot that had killed North had come.

'The killer must have been listening,' said Lowe, his brows puckered into a frown. 'See here, and here' — he pointed to the disturbed earth of a narrow flower-bed — 'this is where he stood.'

'Did you see anybody?' muttered Jim.

The dramatist shook his head.

'No, he'd gone by the time I got here,' he answered. 'He must have made off directly after he had fired the shot.'

'I heard no report,' said McWraith. 'Did you?'

He looked from Lowe to Jim, and they shook their heads.

'He probably used a silencer,' said the dramatist and stooping suddenly he picked up something that was lying by the wall.

'Here is the spent shell,' he remarked; 'so the shot was fired with an automatic.'

He slipped the little brass cylinder into his pocket.

'H'm! Well, it's no good attempting to go after the murderer now, he's had ample time to get away. We may as well go inside.'

He began to walk back to the front door, and Jim and McWraith followed in silence.

The death of North — Jim could not think of him by his real name — before their eyes had come as an unpleasant shock, and they both felt rather sick.

When they reached the dining-room they found that during their absence another person had joined the superintendent and the silent form still stretched motionless on the floor. Mrs. North, her face the colour of old parchment, out of which her coal-black eyes seemed to burn like holes pierced with a red-hot iron, was staring down at her dead husband. Her fingers clutched the back of one of the high chairs with a grip that turned the knuckles to a milky white, and she gave no sign that she had heard them enter.

Hartley was standing by the table, his big face glistening with perspiration, watching her. But he looked up as Lowe came in.

'Did you find anything, sir?' he asked.

'Only the used cartridge and the marks of the man's feet where he had stood,' said the dramatist.

He took the shell from his pocket and held it out.

'You'd better take this,' he continued.

With an obvious effort the superintendent pulled himself together.

'We must send for a doctor,' he muttered. 'Have you a telephone here?'

'Yes, in the hall,' answered Jim. 'I'll show you.'

Hartley followed him out and Lowe went over to Mrs. North.

'Don't you think you had better sit down?' he suggested gently; but she took no notice.

With her breast rising and falling irregularly she continued to stare at the figure on the floor.

'Mrs. North,' said Lowe, raising his voice a little, 'I don't think you had better stop here. Let me take you into the other room.'

She heard him this time and turned slowly, looking at him with a dreadful stare. From outside in the hall came the sound of Hartley's deep tones inquiring for a number.

'Dead,' said the woman tonelessly. 'Dead.'

Lowe took her gently by the arm.

'Come with me — ' he began, and then the horrible calm of her face broke and she began to laugh.

Her laughter rang through the silent room and floated out into the hall. Sharp, metallic, mirthless.

'Good God!' breathed McWraith with a shiver. 'Stop her, can't you! It's ghastly!'

But she continued to laugh violently, hysterically, as Lowe led her out of the room.

13

Death Calls Again

Doctor Grendon came in answer to Superintendent Hartley's telephone message and made a preliminary examination, pending the arrival of the police surgeon from Hythe. It was very brief, for the bullet which had killed North had been aimed with deadly accuracy and had passed right through the heart.

Lowe had been rather interested to meet the local doctor, and was not impressed. Dr. Grendon was stout, inclined to be assertive, and full of his own importance. And yet behind this blustering manner the dramatist thought he detected something that was very nearly akin to fear.

After he had made his examination of the body and had given his verdict, he accepted with alacrity the drink that Jim offered. And as he raised the glass to his lips his well-kept, fattish hand was none too steady. He caught Lowe's eye watching him and smiled a little dryly.

'Not used to violent death,' he said in his oily voice. 'I'm used to dealing with the opposite in my practice; rather knocked me up.'

It was the obvious explanation of that trembling hand, and in ordinary circumstances Lowe would have accepted it, but he remembered the look in Japper's eyes when he had at first arrived at the Crossed Hands, and wondered. Everybody in this village seemed to be inwardly afraid. There was an undercurrent of hidden terror that was most extraordinary. What was the cause of it, and from whom did it emanate?

'I think it would be just as well if you had a look at the dead man's wife,' he said; 'she had an attack of violent hysteria just before you arrived, and although she's quieter now, I don't think it would do any harm if she had a draught of something.'

Dr. Grendon set down his empty glass.

'I'll go and look at her,' he said shortly. 'Where is she?'

'I took her up to her room,' said Lowe. 'Superintendent Hartley had better go with you. He has the key.'

'Key?' the doctor looked at him quickly. 'Did you lock her in?

Lowe nodded.

'Yes,' he replied, 'in the circumstances I thought it was best.'

'H'm! All right.' Dr. Grendon picked up his bag and crossed to the door. 'Come on, then, Superintendent,' he said.

Hartley joined him and they passed out into the hall.

'Aren't you going to move — it?' said Jim, jerking his head towards the body.

'They can't until the police doctor has seen it,' answered Lowe.

'I wonder what he would have told us,' muttered McWraith, 'if he'd had the chance of speaking?'

'What the dead man at the cross-roads would have told us,' said Lowe grimly. 'They both held the secret of Stonehurst and they both died before they could divulge it. There's just a chance, though, that Mrs. — er — Gillman may know something. I think from her attitude that she does, but it's no good attempting to question her until she's calmer. Then' — he broke off as there came a startled cry and the thudding of heavy feet on the stairs.

He was crossing quickly to the door when it was flung violently open and Hartley appeared on the threshold. He was panting jerkily and his face was drawn.

'Mr. Lowe,' he said with difficulty, 'Mr. Lowe — I wish you'd come up — that woman's dead!'

'What?' Lowe's face set.

'Are you sure?'

'Dr. Grendon says so,' answered the superintendent.

'How did she die?' snapped the dramatist.

'Poisoned herself — there's a bottle on the table beside her.' Hartley was recovering his breath a little.

'I'll come up — you two stay down here,' said Lowe.

He almost ran out into the hall and ascended the stairs three at a time with the superintendent lumbering up behind him. As he reached the open door of a room lately occupied by the Norths Dr. Grendon, who had been bending over the bed, looked round.

'She's quite dead,' he said. 'Case of suicide, I should think.'

Trevor Lowe came in and stood looking down at the woman on the bed. She was lying on her side, and might quite easily have been asleep.

'Why do you think it's a suicide?' he asked, and the doctor shrugged his plump shoulders.

'What else could it have been?' he said irritably; 'the window was fastened and the door was locked — as you know yourself.'

'How did she die?' asked Lowe.

'Veronal; here is the bottle.' The doctor stretched out his hand towards it.

'Don't touch it, please, sir,' rapped Hartley; 'you haven't touched it, have you?'

'As a matter of fact, I have,' answered Grendon. 'I naturally picked it up when we first found there was something wrong.'

'Oh, you did, did you,' put in Lowe. 'Yes, of course, I suppose you would.'

He went over to the window and examined the catch. It was securely fastened, and he noticed that it was a patent catch which could not have been prised up from outside. Also there was no sign of a scratch or mark on its polished surface.

'Was the door locked?' he asked Hartley as he came back to the bed.

The superintendent nodded.

'You're certain?' persisted Lowe.

'Quite, sir,' answered Hartley. 'I unlocked it myself.'

Lowe bit his lower lip.

'It certainly looks like suicide, and yet — '

He bent over the little bedside table and looked at the tiny bottle of white tablets. There were four left.

'How many of these would have been fatal?' he asked.

'They're half-grain tablets,' answered Dr. Grendon. 'Four would have been a fatal dose.'

Lowe looked round him.

'You haven't moved anything from this table?' he said.

Grendon shook his head.

'No,' he answered. 'Why?'

'You'd expect her to have taken them in water,' explained the dramatist, 'but there's no glass within her reach.'

'They're quite easily swallowed without,' Grendon pointed out.

'But most people take these things with water,' muttered Lowe.

'There's a glass of water, over there, sir,' said Hartley; but Lowe had already seen it for himself and was peering into the bottom of the glass.

'Dry,' he said. 'Strange she should have swallowed them without water when there was water so near at hand.'

'Well, she evidently did,' remarked Dr. Grendon testily. 'Really it seems to me to be a clear case of suicide. The window was fastened, the door was locked. Nobody could have got in.'

'Apparently not,' agreed Lowe, but he was frowning. 'Was she lying like that when you found her?' He addressed his question to the superintendent.

'Yes, sir,' answered Hartley. 'I thought she was asleep at first.'

Lowe pinched his chin. It certainly seemed as though the woman must have committed suicide. Nobody could have gained access to that room, and yet there was no denying that if she had known anything her death was very lucky for somebody. Perhaps, though, she had been deeply involved in this sinister business and had realised that she was in danger of arrest. In that case she might quite easily have chosen this way out. Lowe felt angry with himself for having left her alone, but when he had left she had seemed quite calm; perhaps this was the reason. Perhaps she had already made up her mind as to what she was going to do. All the same it would never have happened if he had had the sense to have her watched. It had been a mistake, and he hated making mistakes.

He roused himself from his thoughts to find Hartley and Dr. Grendon watching him.

'Well,' he said, 'there's nothing more we can do at the moment; we may as well lock the door again and go downstairs.'

The doctor appeared to be only too pleased to leave that room of death, and Lowe waited while Hartley shut and locked the door, and then went with him down the stairs.

Jim and McWraith turned eagerly as they came in and demanded to know what had happened. The dramatist told them.

'Poor soul,' said Jim in a hushed voice. 'I wish we hadn't left her alone.'

'I wish we hadn't, too,' said Lowe. 'It was my fault; I ought to have thought of this possibility and taken precautions.'

Dr. Grendon went across to the sideboard and helped himself to a stiff whisky, which he gulped down neat. As he set down the glass the sound of a car coming up the drive sent Hartley out into the hall, and presently he came back with the police doctor, who looked more skinny than ever in the full light of day. He glared at Lowe, shot a quick, inquisitive glance at Grendon, and ignored Jim and McWraith altogether.

'You're having plenty of excitement

round here,' he remarked. 'Two murders in less than forty-eight hours.' He clicked his tongue against his teeth. 'Is this the victim?'

Before anybody could answer him he had dropped on one knee beside the body and was staring shortsightedly at the wound.

'H'm! Death must have been almost immediate,' he said. 'The bullet appears to have mushroomed out and lodged somewhere in the muscles. I don't see any signs of an egress wound. Where did the shot come from?'

Hartley explained.

'Ah, that accounts for it,' he grunted. 'Hitting the glass would make it mushroom. That's why the wound isn't a clean one.'

'I thought that,' remarked Dr. Grendon as the police surgeon glared up at him.

'Did you — did you?' he snapped. 'Are you Dr. Grendon? How do you do? Not much used to this sort of thing, eh?'

'Not at all used to it,' said Grendon a little stiffly.

'Neither am I,' retorted the other, scrambling to his feet, 'but I shall be if they go on at this rate. Homicidal maniac loose in the place, or what?'

'Maybe; we don't know yet,' answered Hartley cautiously. 'Will you come upstairs, now?'

'Upstairs? What for?' demanded Dr. Peters.

'The dead man's wife is upstairs,' said Lowe. 'She appears to have committed suicide.'

'Good God!' Peters' neck protruded from his loose collar until it was an amazing length. 'You don't say so! At this rate the entire population of Stonehurst will be wiped out; not that that'd be much loss.' He bustled over to the door. 'Take me up to the room, Hartley, and let's get it over.'

During the short space of time that the police doctor and the superintendent were away a silence fell over the group in the dining-room. Trevor Lowe, busily occupied with his own thoughts, was standing by the window, staring out at as much of the garden as was visible at this point. Dr. Grendon, plucking nervously at his lips, was gazing at nothing, and Jim and McWraith lounged against the fireplace, watching each in turn. In less than five minutes Dr. Peters and the superintendent came back, and the police doctor confirmed Grendon's diagnosis as to the cause of the woman's death.

'There'll have to be a post mortem, of course,' he said. 'I'll arrange about that at once. Are you ready to have these remains put into the ambulance?'

Hartley nodded, and called to a constable who had come with the ambulance that had brought Peters, and between them they lifted the body of North and carried it out. When his wife had been placed in the vehicle beside all that was left of her husband it drove off with Grendon and the police doctor, and Hartley came back and joined Lowe, Jim and McWraith in the dining-room.

'Well, sir,' he said, 'what do you suggest we do next?'

'I suggest,' said Lowe, 'that we go and arrange with your aunt to put up myself and my secretary for the length of our stay in Stonehurst.'

The superintendent's big face broke

into a smile. 'I'm glad you've decided to leave the Crossed Hands, sir,' he said. 'Somehow I don't think you'd find it very healthy.'

'I don't think anywhere in Stonehurst is going to be very healthy for us during the next few days,' answered the dramatist. 'I'm under the impression that I, in particular, am going to be very unpopular indeed.'

'If you're thinking of shifting from the inn,' put in Jim, 'why not come and stay here?'

Lowe considered.

'Would you mind very much, Hartley?' he said at last.

The superintendent shook his head.

'No, sir,' he said; 'in fact, I think it's a better suggestion than mine.'

'That's settled, then,' exclaimed Jim. 'When will you come?'

'As soon as White comes back from London with our things,' answered Lowe.

But Arnold White did not come back, and it was nearly a week before Trevor Lowe was destined to see his secretary again!

14

White Meets With Trouble

Arnold White reached Portland Place shortly before midday and decided to have lunch before starting out on the return trip to Stonehurst.

While the meal was being prepared he went upstairs and packed his own and Lowe's suitcase with the things that he thought would be necessary for their stay.

After that he shaved and had a bath, for neither of these things had been possible at the Crossed Hands, and came down to find the table laid and his food ready and waiting.

He was ravenously hungry and thoroughly enjoyed the tender steak which was put before him.

By the time he had finished and drunk a cup of coffee it was a little after two o'clock, and he began to think about getting back to Stonehurst.

He carried the suitcases downstairs, said good-bye to the housekeeper, and went out to the waiting car, which he had left drawn up outside the door.

Stowing the bags in the back, he took his place behind the wheel, and as he pressed on the pedal of the self-starter happened to glance at the petrol gauge.

It was very low, and he decided to call in at the garage round the corner, and have the tank filled up.

Lowe used a special mixture of petrol and benzol, and whenever possible White liked to keep to this.

He was a quarter of an hour at the garage, and when he drove out and turned the long radiator of the car in the direction of Oxford Street he failed to notice the leather-clad figure on the motor-cycle who had watched him leave Portland Place and waited while he had made his call at the garage.

There was no reason why he should have noticed this man, for he was not expecting to be followed, and neither did the cyclist attempt to do so after he had come out of the filling-station. Instead he swung his powerful machine round in the opposite direction and drove it slowly up Portland Place, turned to the right at the end, and presently came to a call-office.

Here he left the motor-cycle at the kerb and, entering the scarlet box, was presently engaged in a long conversation with somebody at the other end of the wire.

Had White been able to hear what was being said a great deal of trouble might have been avoided.

But White was at that moment entirely engaged in steering Lowe's Rolls in and out of the stream of traffic in Oxford Street and looking forward to the time when he should have left the outskirts of London behind and be able to let the powerful engine have its head.

He got through the traffic at last, passed the straggling edge of a suburb and came out into open country.

The needle of the speedometer spun round to forty as his foot came down steadily on the accelerator, swung up to fifty, and stayed there quivering.

The afternoon was fine and sunny and the clean sweet air hummed round the wind-screen and brought a glow of colour to his cheeks.

He was rather anxious to get back and learn what had happened — if anything — for this mysterious business interested him immensely.

He tried, as he kept the big car running smoothly along the broad road, to evolve some theory that would account for the disappearances, the killing of the unknown man at the cross-roads, and the attempt on Lowe at the inn that failed.

It was the time lapse between the disappearances of Scory — what was the other man's name: he couldn't remember it — and Drin that baffled him. Those two years had to be taken into account. Whatever was the explanation behind the affair, it was something that had been going on for some time.

He was still puzzling when he reached Maidstone and decided to stop at a cafe for tea.

It was nearly four when he started on the second half of his journey, and by the time he reached Hythe, getting on for half-past five.

He took the coast road from Hythe, the same that Lowe had taken on the previous night, and turned off just before reaching Dymchurch into the secondary road that led through to Stonehurst. This was a lonely, winding country road, bordered on each side by tall hedges, beyond which lay wide stretches of ploughed fields.

Just before reaching the cross-roads where he and Lowe had made their tragic discovery the night before there was an old tumble down cottage, empty because it was in too bad a condition for anyone to have lived in it, for there was nothing except the four walls left.

The roof had fallen in and the windows were glassless; even part of the front wall was in ruins, and the whole place looked as if it might collapse completely at any moment.

White glanced at it as he approached, and then as the car came abreast he heard two loud reports and the wheel in his hand was wrenched round.

He knew what had happened at once — the front tyres had burst.

With an angry exclamation of annoyance he stopped the engine and got out. Both front tyres were as flat as pancakes, and he was wondering what had caused them to go suddenly together like this when he saw.

The roadway had been sprinkled with sharp iron spikes.

'What a damned silly trick!' said White aloud, his face red with anger. 'Whoever did this ought to get six months!'

'Indeed?' said a voice gently. 'I think it's a pretty good trick. It's had the desired effect, anyhow.'

White straightened up and swung round.

A tall figure, clad in a long coat, a handkerchief bound round his nose and mouth, was watching him.

'Who — ' began White furiously; but the stranger interrupted him.

'Put up your hands,' he said evenly, and the secretary saw that he held a small, snub-nosed automatic. 'I've been expecting you for some time. You're late.'

'What the dickens do you think you're playing at?' demanded White hotly.

'I'm not playing at anything,' retorted the other, still in that gentle, almost caressing tone. 'This is not a game, I can assure you. Look behind you.'

White looked and saw three other men emerging from the ruins of the cottage.

Like the man who held the pistol, their faces were concealed by handkerchiefs and they advanced towards him silently.

A thrill of apprehension shot through him. What was the meaning of this ambush?

'We're rather afraid that you and your employer are going to be a nuisance,' said the first man, and he might almost have read White's thoughts. 'So we are taking the precaution of attending to you first and putting you safely out of the way.'

Before White could reply the other three approaching men had reached him. Two gripped his arms and the third, in spite of his struggles, clapped a reeking wad over his nose and mouth.

He tried to hold his breath, but his exertions had made him pant, and he was forced to draw in a gulp of the drug.

He felt his head swim and experienced

a violent desire to be sick. He tried to jerk his head away from the chloroform-soaked pad, but it was pressed tighter. And then his senses were engulfed in a wave of darkness that swept into his brain and receded, carrying with it the last vestige of consciousness.

As he fell back limply into the arms of his captors the man with the pistol advanced.

'Has he gone off?' he inquired; and was answered by a nod from the man with the chloroform. 'Good,' he said. 'Take him over to the cottage and secure him. I'll get rid of the car and come back. So keep him there and wait with him until I do.'

He pocketed the automatic and went over to the car. Getting up behind the wheel, he started the engine and began to drive slowly towards Stonehurst.

The three men left behind picked up the unconscious figure of White and carried it towards the ruins of the cottage.

In a few seconds the road was empty and deserted, and it remained so until ten minutes later, when the tall figure of the man who had driven Lowe's car away reappeared walking rapidly towards the cottage.

His eyes above the handkerchief gave a keen glance round before he forced his way through the tangled bushes and entered the rubbish littered space that the four crumbling walls enclosed.

The three other men had removed the handkerchiefs from their faces and were sitting on a heap of stones, smoking cigarettes.

Arnold White, still unconscious, was lying near by, securely bound and with a gag tied across his mouth.

'We'd better get him away now,' said the man. 'One of you pick up those spikes and then we'll carry him across the field to the car.'

A short, thick-set man with a red face and a stubbly beard threw away his half-smoked cigarette and rose to his feet.

'I'll go and clear up the road,' he said; 'and there's no reason why you should wait for me. You could get along with him to the car and I'll go home, see? Don't you think that's best?'

The tall man nodded.

'Yes,' he answered. 'That's all right. You carry on, then.'

The red-faced man lounged out and the other turned to the two men who were still sitting smoking.

'Come on,' he said; 'pick him up and we'll get away.'

They obeyed, and carrying White's helpless form between them, made their way out of the ruins and across the field at the back.

Passing through a gap in the hedge they came out into a narrow lane where a closed car was waiting.

The tall man opened the door and White was bundled into the back. The two who had carried him got into the front of the car, and one of them slid in behind the wheel and started the engine.

The other man shut the door.

'You know what you've to do,' he said, and they both nodded. 'All right' — he turned away — 'then off you go.'

The car moved forward slowly at first, but with gathering speed, and bumped down the lane.

He stood watching it until it was out of sight, and then, removing the handkerchief from his face, he slipped it into his pocket and walked away in the opposite direction.

15

Vanished!

Trevor Lowe did not begin to worry until after darkness had set in.

After arranging with Jim Winslow to come back as soon as he had collected his secretary, he had gone down to the Crossed Hands and informed the landlord that he had decided not to remain there — a decision that had brought something very like a look of relief to Mr. Japper's pale eyes — paid the bill and ordered tea.

It was served to him by the landlord's daughter in the bar-parlour, and he expected while he drank it that White would turn up at any moment. But there was no sign of him.

He finished his tea and smoked two pipes, but still his secretary had not put in an appearance. And at last he came to the conclusion that something had happened to detain him in town.

It never entered his head there was any cause for alarm. Quite a number of things might be the reason for White's delay in getting back. Letters that had required attending to at once, or perhaps someone had called and had been difficult to shift. Any number of things.

Leaving word with Mr. Japper for White to come up to Greytower, Lowe left the inn and walked back.

Jim and McWraith were in the kitchen when he arrived, engaged in trying to cook something for dinner.

There was a lot of smoke and a great smell of burning, but as far as Lowe could see precious little else.

Jim welcomed him with a grin.

'Do you know anything about steak?' he asked.

'I know that it tastes much better if you don't burn it,' said the dramatist, and seizing the frying-pan from McWraith's hand, he took it off the blazing fire. 'Ugh!' he grunted, looking at the leathery mass of blackness that reposed at the bottom. 'Is this steak?'

'It *was*,' said McWraith, wrinkling his nose. 'I'll admit it doesn't look like it now.'

'It would have been better if you had put some sort of grease in the pan,' said Lowe. 'The only thing you can do with this is to throw it away. What else have you got?'

'There's some bacon and half a dozen eggs,' answered Jim, 'and that's about all.'

'Well, we'll see what we can do with those,' remarked the dramatist, taking off his jacket and rolling up his sleeves.

'Are you going to cook them?' demanded Jim.

Lowe's eyes twinkled.

'I think I'd better, don't you?' he remarked. 'Have either of you ever cooked bacon and eggs before?'

'I haven't,' grunted McWraith.

'Neither have I,' confessed Jim.

'Well, I have,' answered Lowe. 'You fetch them and I'll get on with it. You might get rid of that steak, though,' he added. 'I shall want the pan.'

McWraith carried it away and deposited it in some mysterious place in the scullery, while Jim went in search of the bacon and eggs.

Fifteen minutes later they sat down to an appetising meal in the big stone-flagged kitchen.

'I've never tasted better bacon and eggs,' said Jim, speaking with his mouth full. 'How did you manage it?'

Lowe smiled.

'I've cooked things in all sorts of weird places,' he said, 'and all sorts of weird things, too.'

'Well, I must say you're an expert,' said McWraith, helping himself to a huge chunk of bread.

'Your secretary's a long time, isn't he?' asked Jim. 'Weren't you expecting him back this afternoon?'

'I was, but I expect he's been detained over something,' answered the dramatist.

'You know,' said the new owner of Greytower, 'I shall have to get some kind of servants to take the place of the Norths. What do you think I'd better do?'

'I certainly shouldn't try and get them locally,' advised Lowe. 'I should either have them sent down from London or get them from Hythe.'

'Yes, perhaps you're right,' Jim nodded. 'I'll have to see about it first thing in the morning. We can't go on without anybody.'

They finished their meal, washed up the dirty things and went along to the drawing-room, where McWraith had lighted a fire.

'I can get fires to burn all right,' he said proudly, indicating the cheerful blaze.

'And steaks, too,' murmured Trevor Lowe with a smile.

The huge Scotsman grinned.

They settled down round the fire and began chatting about the excitement of the day. So engrossed did they become that it was with a start of surprise that Lowe suddenly discovered that it was ten o'clock.

For the first time he felt a little twinge of uneasiness at White's absence. What could be detaining him?

'If you don't mind,' he said, rising to his feet, 'I think I'll put a call through to London and find out what time White left.'

'Carry on,' said Jim. 'While you're staying here you can look upon the house as your own.'

Lowe had some difficulty in getting connection, but presently he heard the voice of his housekeeper demanding to know who it was.

Lowe told her.

'Why, he left directly after lunch,' said the woman. 'About half-past two that was.'

The dramatist's face went suddenly grave.

'Half-past two, was it?' he said. 'Thank you.'

He hung up the receiver, and as he turned away from the instrument he was feeling really alarmed.

Arnold White should have reached Stonehurst hours ago. What had happened to him?

His first thought was an accident to the car. But he quickly discarded that possibility. The car could easily have been identified, and the housekeeper would have heard from the police, and the information been relayed to him.

No; the reason for his secretary's non-appearance was due to some other cause.

He went back to the drawing-room, and his face must have shown the anxiety he was feeling, for Jim said quickly:

'What's the matter?'

Lowe explained, and both McWraith and his friend looked uneasy.

'What can have happened to him?' muttered Jim.

'That's what I'm wondering,' said Lowe. 'Do you remember my telling you about those Scotland Yard men who disappeared — ?'

'Good God!' broke in McWraith, his florid face a shade paler. 'You don't think that — '

The end of his sentence was interrupted by the whirring of the telephone bell, and Jim, leaping to his feet, went out into the hall.

They heard him lift off the receiver and inquire who was speaking, and then in a louder voice call:

'Mr. Lowe! Superintendent Hartley wants you.'

Lowe was at his side almost before he had finished speaking and had taken the receiver from his hand.

'Hallo!' he said. 'This is Trevor Lowe. What is it, Hartley?'

'A constable on patrol duty has just reported having found your car, sir,' answered the gruff voice of Hartley. 'It was standing deserted on a piece of waste ground just outside Stonehurst. He examined it and found your name and address. Do you know anything about it?'

'I don't,' said Lowe grimly. 'But there's a lot I want to know. He didn't see anything of my secretary, did he? He ought to be with that car.'

'There was nobody with it,' answered the Superintendent; 'nothing but two suitcases, sir.'

'Where are you?' asked the dramatist.

'I'm at the station at Hythe, sir,' was the reply. 'The constable's report came through to the sergeant ten minutes ago, and when I heard I thought I'd better ring you up.'

'I'm glad you did,' said Lowe. 'Where is the car now?'

'Where it was found, sir — the constable's with it. I told him to go back and keep an eye on it until I had phoned you.'

'All right, Hartley; thanks,' said Lowe. 'I'll go along there now.'

He put the receiver back on the hook and turned to Jim and McWraith, who had been listening.

'Will you drive me along to the place?' he asked after he had given a résumé of Hartley's conversation.

'Of course,' answered Jim. 'Come along.'

He pulled on a coat and opened the front door.

The garage was round on the opposite side to the Tower, and with Lowe's help he very soon had the doors open and the car out.

They picked up McWraith as they swept round into the drive, and that huge man perched himself on the back.

It took them some little time to find the exact place where the car had been abandoned, in spite of Hartley's directions. But they found it at last — a triangular piece of waste land near the cross-roads — and Lowe made himself known to the constable on guard.

'I only found it meself by accident like,' said the man, 'thought I heard somethin' movin', and flashed on me light. It was a rabbit what I'd 'eard, but the light fell on the car, an' I went to see what it was all about.'

Lowe pulled out his own torch and shone it on the stranded machine.

There was no sign of it being damaged at all, and he switched on the lights. They glowed blindingly.

And then Jim who had been walking round the car uttered an exclamation.

'Why both the front tyres are flat,' he exclaimed.

Lowe stooped and examined them and quickly found the cause of the punctures. In one of them, buried in the tread, was a metal spike.

'This was no accidental puncture,' he said. 'The road must have been strewn with these things for both tyres to have gone.'

His voice was hoarse and strained with

anxiety, and straightening up, he made a hasty search of the interior of the car.

But he found nothing. There was no sign of any violence — nothing at all abnormal except those two flat tyres.

Neither was there anything to show what had happened to Arnold White. Like Locker, Scory and the other two Scotland Yard men, he had disappeared completely and without trace.

16

The Warning

Long after the last light in the cottages and houses of Stonehurst that night had gone out, long after the Crossed Hands had closed its door on the departing figure of its last customer, a hastily organised search party, headed by Superintendent Hartley and Lowe, beat the woods and the thickets and searched the fields and lanes for some trace of Arnold White.

Every available constable that could be spared had been rushed over from Hythe to assist the seekers, and their lanterns, like great glow-worms, flickered and danced here and there in the darkness of the night.

Dawn came greyly, paling the light of the torches and showing up the haggard lines on the face of Trevor Lowe, the heavy pouches beneath the eyes of

Hartley, and the anxiety in the eyes of Jim Winslow and Ian McWraith.

But it brought with it nothing else. No sign of White, alive or dead.

One thing only had been discovered, and this had been found by Lowe himself in the ruins of a tumbledown cottage near the place where the car had been abandoned.

It was nothing much, only three half-smoked cigarettes of a cheap and popular brand. But they had been fresh, and showed that someone had been there recently.

It was quite probable that they had no connection at all with the disappearance of White, but Lowe had picked them up and put them in an old envelope in case they should prove useful later. And that was the entire result of the night's search.

At eight o'clock, tired and dispirited, and full of vague fears, they went back to Greytower.

McWraith made some coffee, while Lowe, Hartley and Jim discussed the situation.

'It looks very serious to me, sir,' said

Hartley gravely. 'There's no doubt that those punctures were made deliberately in order to stop the car.'

Lowe nodded.

'I agree with you,' he said. 'The question is, what happened after the car was stopped? White wouldn't have let himself be overpowered without a struggle, and there is no trace of violence.'

'It seems more than likely,' suggested Jim, 'that if the tyres had suddenly burst with no apparent reason he would have got out to find the cause — '

'And was set upon,' Lowe concluded as he paused. 'Yes, I think that's what must have happened.'

He took the cup of steaming coffee that McWraith handed to him and sipped gratefully at its contents.

'Well, I don't know what we can do next, sir,' said the superintendent, vainly trying to stiffle a prodigious yawn.

'I'm afraid at present we can do nothing,' answered the dramatist wearily. 'The thing we ought to do is to get some sleep.'

Hartley smiled a little wanly.

'I shan't be able to get any sleep, sir,' he said. 'The inquest on that fellow who was shot at the cross-roads is fixed for ten o'clock, and I shall have to go and attend to the preliminaries.'

Lowe started.

In the worry and excitement following the disappearance of White he had forgotten all about the inquest.

'I've got a subpoena for that,' he said. 'It was brought to me at the inn yesterday. There was one for White, too.'

'It's being held in the village hall,' said Hartley. 'But I shall have to go back to Hythe.'

He gulped down his coffee, found that it was hotter than he thought, and gasped.

'I ought to go now, sir, I think,' he spluttered; 'it's getting on for half-past eight.'

'You carry on,' said Lowe. 'We'll see you again at the inquest.'

Hartley departed, and the dramatist, who was feeling almost dead with worry and lack of sleep, went upstairs and had a cold bath.

When he had shaved and changed into another suit from the bags which he had brought back from the car he felt more normal.

His eyes were hot and dry and there was a tight feeling in his head, but the heaviness had gone.

Jim and McWraith followed his example, and when they came back found that Lowe had cooked the breakfast.

By the time they had eaten the meal it was time to set off for the village hall.

'I don't suppose the proceedings will take very long,' said the dramatist as they strode along the road. 'I've no doubt that the police will ask for an adjournment.'

It was just ten when they came to the red-brick building lying back from the High Street, which was the only sign of modernity in Stonehurst, and served the dual purpose of schoolroom and social club.

The coroner had not yet put in an appearance, but the place was already crowded to capacity.

And Lowe looked at the people with interest.

This was the first time he had had an opportunity of seeing the inhabitants of Stonehurst *en masse*. And he decided that they looked a very mixed lot.

The front seats were occupied by what he guessed to be the more important of the residents, and behind these was a sprinkling of men and women whom he found very difficult to place.

They were not villagers; there was nothing of the country about their appearance. And he concluded after a little while that they must be the servants that Hartley had mentioned the newcomers to Stonehurst had brought with them.

Standing about at the back of the hall were the villagers proper. Farmers and their labourers, shopkeepers, etc., and among them the fat unhealthy-faced landlord of the Crossed Hands.

Superintendent Hartley joined him at that moment, and Lowe in a whisper asked him to name the people who were present.

Hartley, still looking tired from his sleepless night, glanced swiftly round.

'That's Lady Thurley with her niece,'

he said in a low voice.

And following the direction of his eyes, Lowe saw a thin elderly woman dressed in black with a harsh eagle-like face, who was sitting bolt upright at one end of the second row of chairs. Beside her was a girl who looked rather uncomfortable.

Behind these two was a man of military appearance, with an iron-grey moustache and hair of the same colour.

He was accompanied by a woman heavily made up, who might have been any age from thirty to fifty.

'They are Mr. and Mrs. Gordon-Watts,' whispered Hartley, 'and the man beside them is Mr. Netherton.'

'Who's the foreign-looking man?' asked Lowe. 'Is that the Frenchman you were talking about?'

The superintendent nodded.

'Yes, Mr. Lucia,' he replied; 'and the fellow behind him is Linney. That's Toogood, that thin-faced man talking to Dr. Grendon.'

Trevor Lowe eyed each of Stonehurst's elite, and came to the conclusion that he did not like any of them.

There was something wrong about them somewhere, and he could not make up his mind what it was. Somehow they did not fit. They should not have been here at all. The place where one would expect to find them was a place like the lounge of a garish, flash hotel in the West End.

As the thought entered his mind he realised with a little inward start what it was that was wrong with them.

They were flashy, that was it — common people, trying to pass themselves off as gentry.

In spite of the smart clothes and the paint and the powder, the origin blazed forth.

There would have been nothing very much in this if they had not all been alike. All stamped with that same blatant trade mark.

Lowe's thoughts were interrupted by the arrival of the coroner and the opening of the proceedings.

Dr. Peters was the first witness called, and he testified in his clear, rather staccato voice, to the cause of death, and after one or two questions the coroner let him go.

Lowe himself was the next witness, and he described in detail how he and Arnold White had discovered the body.

The coroner had evidently been interviewed by the police, for he asked the dramatist no questions at all, but thanked him for his statement and called Superintendent Hartley.

Hartley's evidence was extremely discreet.

He admitted that the identity of the dead man had not yet been discovered, but that the police hoped to be in a position shortly to offer further evidence both in respect to his identity and to the manner in which he had met his death. They were quite certain that it was not a case of suicide, but at this juncture they were not prepared to suggest anybody as having been responsible for the crime.

There were certain clues being followed up, and in the interest of the law he wished to ask the coroner for an adjournment until that day week, to enable further evidence to be collected.

His request was granted after only a slight hesitation on the part of the coroner, and the inquest came to an end.

The coroner collected his notes, had a word or two with the superintendent and a small dapper man, whom Lowe suspected was the chief constable for the district, and departed.

The hall began to clear amid a buzz of conversation, and the dramatist found himself outside with Jim and McWraith.

'Well, that's that,' he remarked.

'Are you coming back to the house with us?' asked Jim, looking about in the hope of catching a glance from Jill Heyford.

Lowe shook his head.

'No,' he replied. 'I want to have a word with Hartley. I'll see you later.'

He saw the superintendent, accompanied by the short, dapper man, making his way towards him, and went to meet them.

'This is Major Winning, the chief constable,' said Hartley. 'Mr. Trevor Lowe, Major.'

The chief constable extended a hand

and gripped the dramatist's.

'How do you do, Mr. Lowe,' he said. 'I rather wanted to have a talk to you. Is there anywhere we can go, Hartley, for a drink?'

'There's only the Crossed Hands, sir,' answered the superintendent, 'and I wouldn't go there if you're going to talk.'

'Suppose we go over to Hythe and have some lunch?' suggested Lowe. 'You've got a car, haven't you, Hartley — '

'He didn't use it this morning,' broke in the chief constable; 'he came over with me in mine, and that's just as good. Let's get along.'

He led the way over to a closed saloon that stood outside the hall.

Several groups of the people who had been present at the brief inquest were still standing about talking, and they eyed the three covertly as they walked towards the car.

'Shall I drive, sir?' asked the superintendent.

'I wish you would,' answered Winning. 'Then I can get in the back and have a talk with Mr. Lowe as we go along.'

Hartley climbed up behind the wheel as Lowe got into the interior with the chief constable.

'Have a cigar?' asked the latter, producing his case as they drove off.

'No, thanks, I'd rather have a pipe, if you don't mind,' said Lowe.

He put his hand into his pocket for his pouch, and in doing so his fingers touched something smooth and square. He drew it out, frowning, and found that it was a sealed envelope.

'How the devil did that get there?' he said aloud, staring at it, and Winning glanced at him quickly.

'Isn't it yours?' he asked.

Lowe shook his head.

'It wasn't there when I went to the inquest,' he declared, 'but it's certainly got my name on it.'

He pointed to the bold 'Trevor Lowe, Esq.,' printed in block letters.

'Why not open it and see what's inside?' suggested the chief constable with a smile.

Lowe slid his thumb under the flap and drew out a single sheet of paper.

After a brief glance he passed it to Major Winning.

'What do you make of that?' he said quietly.

Winning read the message with staring eyes, and his lips pursed into a silent whistle.

Like the envelope, it was printed, and ran:

'GET OUT OF STONEHURST IF YOU WANT TO LIVE. THIS IS THE ONLY WARNING YOU WILL GET.'

There was no signature.

'I wonder which of the people present at the inquest put that into my pocket?' said Trevor Lowe softly.

17

Gathering Shadows

Night came down on Stonehurst with a white, cold mist that filled the lanes and narrow streets and spread out over the fields and meadows like heavy frozen steam.

It was a ground-mist only, for the sky above was clear; moonless, but with many stars.

In the majority of the cottages and houses the lights had long since been put out. But here and there a window gleamed blearily through the swirling vapour, showing that a few at least of the inhabitants were still wakeful.

In Dr. Grendon's neat little house by the green, in the White House, in the Lodge, and further away in the Bungalow. There were lights also at Wood Dene, shining from the window of Lady Thurley's big bedroom; and on the outskirts of the village in the Martins' cottage which had been rented by Mr. Lucia.

In the dark mass of Greytower, rising out of the sea of thin fog that enswathed it, there was no light, for Jim Winslow, Trevor Lowe and Ian McWraith had gone to bed early to make up the sleep they had missed on the night before.

The cracked bell in the church chimed out two, and as the sound faded away into the darkness of the night a figure came slinking down the empty High Street.

It moved silently, with no sound of footfall, and might have been a shadow on the mist but for the glowing end of a cigarette that hung from its lower lip.

Down the slope of the street it went, and vanished in the blackness at the end.

Apparently it was not the only living thing abroad that night, for shortly after its disappearance other figures, moving as noiselessly as the first, began making their way from all directions towards the place at which the first had vanished.

This nocturnal activity went on for nearly twenty minutes after the striking of the church clock, and then the streets of the old village became again deserted.

But the lights no longer glimmered in the windows of the houses where they had before. Darkness now was everywhere. Darkness and the ever thickening mist that rose higher each moment, until at last it even blotted out the tower of Greytower.

And yet the village was not entirely sleeping.

At the bottom of the High Street, past the old forge, stood a low-roofed house, half-cottage and half-bungalow. And in the cosy living-room lights were burning brightly.

Heavy curtains, however, masked the windows, and not a stray ray of light was allowed to penetrate into the misty night.

It was a very comfortable room, this long low ceilinged apartment, with its polished refrectory table and its easy chairs and loungers.

Lit by shaded petrol-vapour lamps and warmed by the cheerful flames of a coal fire, it was comfortable but rather overcrowded, for there were eight people present.

Lady Thurley, her sharp eagle-like face turned towards the fire so that the red glow outlined her thin cheeks and high bridge of her rather hooked nose, was seated in a low chair. She was still dressed in black, but a black that was slightly more festive than that which she had worn at the inquest.

Facing her and smoking a cigarette in a long green holder, sat Mrs. Gordon-Watts, and now it was no longer obscured by a hat her hair showed the dye by which it retained its spurious gold. Her hands were thick and badly shaped, and the red enamel with which her nails were daubed did nothing to add to their beauty. She was dressed in an unnecessarily low-cut evening gown of a hard scarlet that fitted tightly to her plump figure, and on a low table by her side was a glass more than half filled with whisky, to which a very little soda had been added.

On the rim of it was a crescent-shaped red smear where the crimson of her lips had come off.

Her husband, his hands in the pockets of his velvet smoking-jacket, was perched on the arm of a deep settee, talking in a low voice to Dr. Grendon, who was sitting leaning back, looking up at him.

The doctor's fat face was sullen, his thick lips set in a petulant expression.

On the other side of the room stood a group of three men, each holding a half-empty glass and carrying on a discussion in the same low tones as their host.

The thin, almost emaciated Mr. Toogood was doing most of the speaking.

Linney and Netherton were listening and were occasionally interposing a negative or an affirmative as the occasion demanded.

Seated on his own was Mr. Japper, his eyes a little glassy and bloodshot, and rather obviously suffering from the influence of too much of the refreshment he dispensed at the Crossed Hands.

It was not, apparently, a very happy party.

The two women by the fireplace were silent, each covertly watching the other when she was not being observed, and then pretending that she was looking at something else altogether.

Suddenly Mr. Japper's husky voice broke the sibilant whispering that was the only sound in the room.

'He's late,' he said thickly.

Six heads turned towards him, only Lady Thurley remained staring into the fire, and took no notice of the remark.

'Better tell him so,' snapped Dr. Grendon, eyeing Mr. Japper disfavourably.

'I will,' answered the landlord of the Crossed Hands. 'It shows lack of con — con — consideration.'

He managed with difficulty to get the word out.

'You're in a fine state, aren't you?' said Gordon-Watts disgustedly.

Mr. Japper shot him a venomous glance.

'I'm all right,' he said. 'You mind your own business.'

'Let him alone.' Mrs. Gordon-Watts looked round at her husband and frowned.

He shrugged his shoulders and continued his muttered conversation with Dr. Grendon.

It was nearly half-past two by the jade clock on the mantelpiece when there came a soft knocking on the front door.

The low hum of conversation between Gordon-Watts and the doctor stopped abruptly.

'There he is,' muttered Grendon, and rose to his feet.

There was a footfall in the hall and the sound of a door being opened. A short silence, and then a tap on the door of the room in which the eight people were gathered.

'Come in,' said Mr. Gordon-Watts.

A short thick-set man, apparently a servant, opened the door and ushered into the room a tall thin figure that wore a soiled mackintosh buttoned up to the throat and beneath the brim of whose hat showed a black expanse of silk.

The newcomer advanced a few steps into the room, and as the servant closed the door began to speak.

The voice was low and monotonous, pitched on one note, and sounded curiously inhuman.

'I am late,' he said briefly, but made no sort of apology, 'and I can't stay very long to-night, so let's get our business over as quickly as possible.'

Gordon-Watts pulled out a chair by the table, and the man in the mackintosh sat down, making no effort either to remove the hat he was wearing or to undo the closely buttoned coat.

'Let's hear from you first, Toogood,' he went on. 'You got that fellow White all right?'

The emaciated man nodded.

'Yes,' he answered, 'it was easy.'

'There was no hitch? Nothing went wrong?' asked the other quickly.

Toogood shook his head.

'No, everything went according to plan,' he said. 'Smithson phoned me to say he had left London, and we waited for him by the ruined cottage.'

The masked man gave a grunt of approval.

'What do you want us to do with him?' asked Toogood. 'At present I've got him at my place.'

'Keep him there for the moment,' was the reply. 'I haven't made up my mind yet. But I think he may be more useful alive. He's quite safe where he is; there's no chance of his getting away?'

'Not a hope,' said Toogood cheerfully. 'My house is pretty old. They built cellars well in those days.'

'That's all right then.' The eyes behind the slits in the mask glanced keenly round, and fixed themselves on Japper. 'Japper!' The voice became harsh and metallic, and Mr. Japper jumped out of the semi-stupor into which he had sunk. 'What do you mean by coming here in that state?'

The landlord blinked and passed a stubby hand across his mouth.

'I'm all righ',' he muttered thickly.

'You're as near drunk as doesn't matter,' snapped the other. 'This is the second time you've turned up like that, and it'll be the last. You understand?'

'All righ',' growled Japper, but his eyes were angry and his mouth sullen.

'And you can take that look off your face,' said the masked man. 'You've been drinking too much lately, and men who drink are dangerous. Cut it out — or there'll have to be a new landlord at the Crossed Hands.'

Mr. Japper's heavy flaccid face paled until it looked like a bladder of lard.

'I'm sorry,' he whined shakily. 'I 'ad one or two extra drinks with the boys — '

'Well, see that it doesn't happen again,' snapped the other. 'We've got to be extra careful at the moment. The village is notorious — the very thing we wanted to avoid.'

'I'm afraid the North business did a lot of harm that way.' Mr. Netherton passed a well manicured hand across the top of his head and smoothed down his thin reddish hair. 'But it was the lesser of two evils; in another second he would have squealed.'

'You did the only thing that was possible,' agreed the masked man. 'And while I think of it, somebody must keep Lowe under observation always. You'd better fix that up amongst yourselves. It won't, I hope, be necessary for long.'

He turned and looked at Dr. Grendon.

'Tell me,' he went on, 'did that woman — North's wife — commit suicide or didn't she?'

'She did not,' answered Grendon slowly.

'I thought it was rather a lucky coincidence. How did you manage to silence her?'

'She had — luckily — taken a dose of veronal to quieten her nerves,' said Grendon, 'and when Hartley unlocked the door she was asleep. I saw my chance and took it. I pretended that she was already dead and sent him downstairs. While he was gone I gave her a shot of dope from a syringe I had in my bag.'

'H'm! That was risky,' remarked the masked man, and Grendon grunted.

'Not so risky as letting her talk,' he answered. 'She knew as much as her husband did.'

'Well, the danger has been averted, and that's something,' was the reply. 'What we've got to concentrate on now is to avoid any possibility of its recurrence.'

'If you mean taking precautions against any of the men squealing,' put in Gordon-Watts, 'I don't think you need worry. They won't dare to think of it after what's happened — it's done that much good.'

'I wasn't thinking of the men,' said the

other. 'I was thinking of this infernal Lowe fellow. We've got to get rid of him. He's our greatest danger.'

'Well, it shouldn't be difficult.' Mrs. Gordon-Watts removed the long holder from her lips and spoke in a soft husky voice. 'Why not do the same as we did before — with the others?'

'I have already considered that,' said the man in the mask, 'and I think that possibly it will be the best way. But if Lowe disappears we must provide some reason for his disappearance. A reason that will prove acceptable to the world in general, otherwise we shall only precipitate what we are so anxious to avoid and bring the police down here like flies.'

He tapped thoughtfully with his gloved hand on the polished surface of the table.

'Why can we not finish the whole thing?' broke in the deep voice of Lady Thurley, speaking for the first time. 'We have made a considerable amount of money. Why tempt fate by going on?'

'Getting cold feet, Elizabeth?' asked Mrs. Gordon-Watts with a sneer.

'No, merely being sensible,' retorted

the other woman. 'A pitcher can go too often to the well.'

Mrs. Gordon-Watts took a long drink of her whisky and set the glass down with a bang.

'There's no need to start dragging quotations into the matter,' she said. 'I, for one, don't see any reason why we should give up. We may have made money — we have — but it's got to be split up among so many that we can still do with a lot more. Things are not so terribly desperate, anyway. Nobody suspects any of us; they just think there's something going on, but they don't know what, and I don't see why they ever should know, if we're sensible.'

'I entirely agree with you.' The man in the mackintosh shifted round in his chair. 'To give up now, after the difficulties we have surmounted, would be ridiculous. We have succeeded beyond our original hopes, and there is no doubt that we shall do even better in the future.'

'Well,' said Lady Thurley, 'I have merely offered my advice.'

'I don't require advice,' snapped the

other sharply. 'We shall continue with our plans.'

He turned to Gordon-Watts.

'Now let's get on with the business. You have all the reports for last week?'

Gordon-Watts nodded and produced a small attaché case. Laying it on the table, he took a bunch of keys from his pocket and unlocked it.

As he took out a heap of papers and placed them before the man at the head of the table the others gathered round, pulling up their chairs until they were grouped on either side of the oblong strip of polished wood.

The whole scene was rather reminiscent of a board meeting, with the exception of the masked figure who presided.

He carefully examined the documents which had been placed before him and for over an hour and a half he talked and issued orders, while the others listened and made occasional notes.

Presently he collected the papers together and handed them to Gordon-White, who replaced them in the leather case.

'That's that,' he remarked, rising to his feet. 'We shall all meet again at the same time at your house, Mr. Linney, on Monday next. In the meantime, if you wish to communicate anything of importance to me, will you do so in the usual way? Good night!'

Gordon-Watts accompanied him to the front door, while the others prepared to take their departure.

'Watch that woman Thurley,' whispered the masked man as Gordon-White half opened the door. 'She's getting restive, and she may be dangerous.'

'She dare not do much; she's too deeply involved herself,' answered the grey-haired man.

'All the same, watch her,' said the other, and passed out into the misty night.

The figure of a man who had been crouching under the window of the living-room straightened up as his footsteps crunched softly on the gravel path and noiselessly began to follow him.

He followed him as far as a car, which was standing without lights in a lane near the house, watched him get in, and was still watching when the car moved away and vanished in the white fog.

And when he turned away his face was very grave and thoughtful, for with the help of a small chink in the curtain and a microphone which he had pressed against the glass of the window he had both seen and heard everything that had taken place in the White House that night!

18

A Conference at the Yard

The Chief Commissioner leaned back in his chair at the head of the long table in the conference room at Scotland Yard and surveyed the men he had summoned to this meeting.

Three of the four chief constables who each control a different area of London were present — grey-haired elderly men who knew everything there was to be known about police work and who had mostly graduated to their present positions from the ranks — and a scattering of lesser lights in the persons of Chief Inspector Watling and Superintendent Lane — both of the Big Four — Detective Inspector Murley and Detective Sergeant Rawling.

It was ten o'clock in the morning, and outside over the river the fog hung greyly, making the tugboats hoot monotonously as they warned each other and other craft of their approach.

It was just possible to see across the wide thoroughfare of the Embankment, but that was all.

'I've no doubt, gentlemen,' began Sir George Chapple, after a preliminary cough, 'that you have all of you guessed the reason for this conference this morning.'

He paused and looked from face to face, and one of the chief constables nodded.

'It's in connection with this increasing outbreak of crime,' he said gruffly.

'Yes,' the Chief Commissioner sat forward with a peculiar little jerk and rested his wrists on the edge of the table in front of him 'I have all the reports here' — he tapped a pile of bulky folders at his side — 'and I have been going through them carefully. During the past eighteen months there appears to have been a successful attempt at organised crime on a scale that has not hitherto been known, and a serious attempt must be made to check it.'

Chief Inspector Watling looked up from the pencil he had been rolling up and down his blotting-pad.

'Are you referring to the increase in the dope traffic, sir?' he asked.

'Not entirely, Chief Inspector,' answered the Chief Commissioner. 'I am referring to crime in general. There has, as you know, been a marked increase in the traffic in dangerous drugs. It has been the more marked since we were on the point of stamping it out altogether. We had, or we thought we had until lately, succeeded in preventing opium, cocaine, and similar preparations being illegally imported into this country. But recently somebody has contrived to do this on a large scale, in spite of the vigilance of the police. But that is not all' — he drew a folder towards him, opened it, and flicked over the typewritten pages it contained. 'From all over the country there have been complaints of spurious notes in circulation; Bank of England and Treasury notes so skilfully forged that only an expert can detect them from the genuine article. During the past year there has been a succession of large robberies, the perpetrator, or perpetrators of which have so far escaped detection, and in several instances we have become aware of a systematic attempt to levy blackmail upon the most important people in the land. Naturally, we only know the few cases who have had the courage to come forward and make complaints, but there must be a greater number who have suffered, and paid, in silence.'

'You are of the opinion, sir,' asked Watling, as Sir George stopped speaking, 'that these things are connected?'

'I am,' said the Chief Commissioner. 'I have considered the matter carefully, and I have come to the conclusion that there is an unknown and carefully organised — er — gang at work.'

'You are not suggesting, surely,' said one of the chief constables, 'that the master criminal beloved of fiction has made his appearance in real life?'

Sir George shrugged his shoulders.

'I am only suggesting,' he replied, 'that this sudden flood of crime is due to systematic organisation. Who is responsible for that organisation I don't know.'

'There is certainly no doubt, sir,' put in Superintendent Lane, 'that this drug traffic is being handled very smartly.

I've been in charge of the matter and I haven't been able to find a vestige of a clue as to who is distributing the stuff.'

'How does it reach the addicts?' asked the grey-haired chief constable who had spoken before.

'Through the usual 'runners',' answered Lane. 'We've pulled in a lot of them, but the trouble is that they can't tell us where they get the stuff from. All that we can get out of them is that they buy it at so much an ounce from a man who arranges to meet them at night, usually on a lonely road, and never twice at the same place. He comes in a car, hands over the parcel of drugs, receives payment and clears out. He's the fellow we want.'

'And the 'slush' notes are circulated in the same way,' said Chief Inspector Watling. 'The fellows who pass it buy it in bulk. There's no doubt that there's some sort of a criminal organisation at work.'

'But ruled over by a master mind?' The chief constable shook his grizzled head. 'You're not asking us to believe that, Watling?'

'I know it sounds absurd, sir,' replied

Watling, 'but I believe that it's the case. I've gone very deeply into the matter and I've made one or two very curious discoveries.'

He drew a folder towards him and opened it.

'In the first place, several known crooks who have specialised in the drug traffic — the bigger people, I mean, not the little touts — have completely disappeared from their usual haunts, and we haven't been able to trace them. In the second place, according to reports I've had, a number of 'slush' men have also vanished. When this flood of dud notes began to come to our notice I put my finger on three men who might be the artists, and had 'em traced. One of them, Nevinsky, was in prison, but the other two, Freeman and Kenner, couldn't be found. They haven't been seen for months.'

'The same thing has happened in connection with these burglaries, sir,' said Detective Inspector Murley. 'I investigated the last three and I came to the conclusion that they were the work of one man — Johnny Calling. I sent out to have him pulled in, but he couldn't be found anywhere.'

'Do you mean that all these men have completely disappeared?' asked the third chief constable, a younger man than the other two, who had not previously spoken.

'Completely, sir,' answered Inspector Murley.

'What steps have been taken to find them?' asked the Chief Commissioner.

'The usual, sir,' said Murley. 'A description has been circulated to all stations, and men have been put on to make inquiries.'

'And you've been unable to trace them?' Sir George shook his head. 'That's unfortunate, Inspector; something must be done about it.'

'We're doing all we can, sir,' said Murley. 'We've got several 'noses' — er — police informers, sir, keeping their eyes and ears open. That, I think, is the most likely chance of hearing anything.'

'That is, of course, always supposing that these men are still in the country,' remarked the chief constable who had been sceptical concerning Sir George's suggestion of a master criminal. 'If they have succeeded in getting out of the country — abroad — you're not likely to hear any more of them.'

'I don't think they've done that, sir,' put in Chief Inspector Watling. 'We've made extensive inquiries at all the ports, and we haven't found out anything that tends to show these men might have escaped abroad.'

'But you've no proof that they haven't?' grunted the chief constable. 'It seems to me that it's more than likely, since there's no trace of them to be found in this country. If there *is* in existence an organisation of the kind that Sir George has suggested, it seems to me a great deal more likely that it is being worked from abroad than in this country.'

'I'll communicate with the French Sûreté,' said Watling, making a note, 'and the Belgian and German police.'

'I think it would be worth while,' said the Chief Commissioner. 'Something must be done to put a stop to this crime epidemic. What has been done at present is most unsatisfactory: most unsatisfactory indeed.'

'I assure you, sir,' said Watling a little stiffly, 'that everything has been done that could be done.'

'I'm not suggesting that it hasn't,' broke in Sir George. 'But what is being done at present is obviously not sufficient. There must be a general tightening up all round. This organisation must be found and broken up. Now let us go through all the reports that we have and see if they will not suggest to us a fresh line of inquiry.'

They went through all the reports. Watling, in a rather bored manner, because he had read them over and over again with the same object.

But they found nothing on which to base a fresh line of inquiry.

Until one o'clock they argued and discussed the matter, and when the meeting finally broke up had come to no satisfactory conclusion.

Inspector Murley on his way back to his uncomfortable office ran into Shadgold in the corridor.

'Hallo, Murley,' said Shadgold; 'you're looking pretty glum. What's the matter?'

'I've just wasted three hours that might have been put to more profitable use,' answered Murley savagely.

Shadgold grinned.

'Been up before the heads?' he asked.

Murley nodded.

'Yes, about this increase of crime business,' he said. 'The Old Man' — in this disrespectful way he referred to Sir George Chapple — 'has got an idea in his head that it's the work of an organised gang.'

Shadgold's smile broadened.

'What's the matter with him?' he said. 'Been reading sensational novels?'

'I don't know that there mayn't be something in it,' said Murley. 'Watling seems to agree with him, and he's in charge of the case.' He frowned. 'There's certainly a lot that's similar in the way the drug traffic and the 'slush' notes are being worked. And these burglaries, too.'

'I'm glad I'm not on the job,' said Shadgold. 'Are you working with Watling?'

'Yes,' answered Murley with a grimace.

'What are you on now?'

'Trying to find out what happened to Locker and those other fellows,' said Shadgold. 'Got hauled back from my holiday to do it.'

'I wish you luck,' said Murley, unsympathetically. 'In a way we're both trying to do the same thing.'

'How do you mean?' Shadgold looked surprised. 'There's no connection that I can see.'

'There's no connection that *I* can see,' retorted Murley, 'except that you're trying to find four detectives that have disappeared and I'm trying to find four crooks that have disappeared.'

'Who are they?' asked Shadgold.

'Freeman and Kenner, the zinc scratchers,' answered Murley. 'Johnny Calling, the — '

'Did you say Johnny Calling?' broke in Shadgold quickly.

'Yes,' Murley's thin face was surprised. 'Why?'

'Well, you needn't look for him any longer,' said Shadgold. 'I can tell you where to find him.'

'You can?' said Murley eagerly. 'Where?'

'On a marble slab in the mortuary at Hythe,' answered Shadgold. 'An unknown man was found murdered at the four cross-roads just outside Stonehurst the other night, and the Hythe police sent his prints up to the Yard to see if they could identify them.'

'And was he — ' Inspector Murley began the needless question, and Shadgold interrupted him.

'He was the fellow you're looking for,' he said. 'Johnny Calling!'

19

Shadgold Arrives

Superintendent Hartley brought the news of the dead man's identity to Trevor Lowe shortly after the dramatist had finished breakfast.

'Johnny Calling, eh?' remarked Lowe. 'So that's who it was. I wondered why his face seemed familiar.'

'Did you know him then, sir?' asked Hartley in surprise.

Lowe shook his head.

'I can't say that I knew him,' he replied. 'At least, not well. But I was introduced to him once at a night-club. I was looking for types for a film-play I was working on, and the man who took me to this club introduced me to Calling. I remember thinking at the time that it was rather a peculiar name.'

'According to his record he was a burglar,' said the superintendent, 'and a pretty clever one. He's only been convicted once.'

'When did you hear about him?' asked Lowe.

'It came through this morning, sir,' answered Hartley. 'If you didn't know the man well it's certainly rather funny that he should try to make that appointment with you.'

He wrinkled his brows in a puzzled manner.

'I wish I knew what it was he was going to say.'

'So do I,' agreed the dramatist. 'If we knew that this business would be over, Hartley. I suppose there's no news of my secretary?'

Hartley shook his large head.

'None at all, sir, I'm sorry to say,' he replied. 'The search is still going on, though. I've put all the available men I could spare on to it.'

Lowe bit hard on the stem of his pipe.

Although he tried not to show it he was terribly worried. In spite of his long night's rest, he looked as if he had not slept for weeks. Sheer physical exhaustion had made him sleep, but it had been a broken rest, troubled by unpleasant dreams, in which Arnold White had been the central figure. There was a bond of friendship between himself and his secretary that is not usually found between employee and employer.

White was the son of an old friend of Lowe's who had been killed in the war. And for this reason, if for nothing else, he felt a certain amount of responsibility concerning him.

That he had come up against the menace that lurked at the heart of the outwardly peaceful village of Stonehurst, there was little doubt. But what had happened to him? Lowe was dreadfully afraid — he only admitted this to himself — that he was dead.

It was true no body had been found, but neither had the bodies of Locker, Scory and the other men who had been snatched into oblivion. And yet it was unlikely that any of them were alive.

The superintendent, watching him across the big dining-room at Greytower, guessed what was passing in his mind and tried rather clumsily to offer consolation.

'I shouldn't start thinking the worst yet, sir,' he said gruffly. 'There's a chance he may only have been kidnapped.'

He thought there was very little chance of that in his own mind, but he had taken a liking to this pleasant-faced man before him and wanted to make the prospect sound as cheering as possible.

'I sincerely hope that what you say is the case,' muttered Lowe. 'But I very much doubt it. So do you really. When are you holding the inquest on the Norths?' He changed the subject abruptly, and Hartley felt rather relieved.

'To-morrow, sir,' he answered, 'at ten. We shall only take the medical evidence, and then ask for an adjournment, the same as we did with Calling.'

'But has — ' began Lowe, and stopped as the door was flung open and the huge figure of Ian McWraith burst in, flourishing a tea-cloth in one hand and a small object in the other.

'Jim found this!' he cried, 'in one of the canisters on the kitchen mantelpiece.'

'What is it?' asked the dramatist,

stretching out his hand.

'It's a key, Mr. Lowe,' said the voice of Jim Winslow, as he appeared in the doorway behind his friend. 'We ran out of tea and I was looking to see if there was any in those cans on the mantelpiece, and I found it.'

Lowe took the key from McWraith's fingers and looked at it.

It was not a very large one, and was by no means new, although it had been carefully cleaned and freshly oiled.

'I wonder if it's the key that fits the lock of that door in the Tower,' he muttered.

'That's what I thought it might be,' said Jim quickly.

'Well, we can soon find out,' remarked the dramatist. 'Let's go along there now and see.'

He led the way out into the hall and went along to the kitchen with the others following him.

Reaching the Tower room, he crossed to the door, and switching on his torch, inserted the key in the lock.

It fitted perfectly, and with a twist of his wrist he turned it.

With the three others crowding on his heels, Lowe stepped across the threshold and found himself in a small oblong apartment of stone that was obviously, from its size and shape, built into the thickness of the Tower wall.

So far as furniture went it was quite empty. But in one corner there was a heap of folded blankets, and near it a hurricane lamp.

There was no window, and the place was rather like a prison cell.

Lowe flashed his light about and then let the beam rest on a spot on the floor midway between the back wall and the door.

'Look at that,' he said grimly. 'I don't think there can be any doubt that this is where Calling met his death.'

Hartley peered over his shoulder at the dark irregular stain on the grimy flags that formed the floor.

'That's where he must have fallen after he had been shot,' Lowe went on. 'We should find the bullet somewhere about if we look carefully.'

He began to spray the walls with the

ray from his torch, and presently he found what he was looking for — a star splash of white on the old stonework.

'Here's where the bullet struck,' he said, pointing it out to the others, 'and it probably rebounded.'

He turned his attention to the floor, but it was Jim who found the small piece of misshapen lead.

It was lying near the heap of blankets, and he picked it up.

'That's a fairly conclusive clue,' remarked Lowe, twisting it about between his finger and thumb. 'This is where Calling was shot.'

Hartley scratched his head.

'What I'd like to know,' he muttered, 'is who shot him?'

'That's what we'd all like to know,' said the dramatist. 'It may have been North, but if it was, I think he was acting on somebody else's instructions.'

'You'd better look after this,' he said.

Hartley put the little piece of battered metal carefully away in his pocket.

'It looks as if somebody had slept here,' said Jim, eyeing the pile of folded blankets. 'I can't think of any other reason for those.'

Lowe nodded.

'That's what I think,' he agreed. 'Although I doubt if they slept here willingly.'

'What do you mean, sir?' asked Hartley.

'It looks very much to me as if this place had been used for a prison,' answered the dramatist. 'It would be ideal for that purpose, for the thickness of the walls and the door would make it practically soundproof.'

'But who could the prisoner have been?' demanded Ian McWraith.

'I haven't the least idea,' said Lowe. 'Perhaps there was more than one. This may have been a kind of condemned cell and execution shed combined. Look there, and there.' He pointed to two separate places on the floor. 'Those stains are not as fresh as the others, but they are obviously bloodstains.'

Jim gave a little shudder.

'You think other people besides Calling were killed here?' he asked hoarsely.

'I think it seems likely,' replied Lowe.

'It wouldn't surprise me to know that those poor fellows from the Yard had spent the last hours of their lives here.'

'How — horrible!' Jim's face was paler than it had been when he had first entered that cell-like apartment. 'For God's sake let's get out of the place!'

He stumbled towards the door.

'I don't think there's much more we can learn here,' said Lowe, glancing quickly round. 'So we may as well lock the place up again.'

They came out of the room with its signs of violent death, and after carefully locking the door Lowe gave the key into Hartley's keeping.

'Well, sir,' remarked the superintendent as they made their way back to the dining-room, 'it's been interestin', but I don't see that it's got us much farther.'

'I'm afraid it hasn't,' said Lowe gravely. 'And I'm not at all certain that anything will. We're up against some very clever people, and they have the advantage, inasmuch as they know us but we don't know them. So far as I can see the only thing to do is to wait until they make some further move, and hope that they will give themselves away. There's one thing that seems rather promising, and that is that they're scared.'

'Scared?' Hartley looked at him questioningly.

'Yes; the attempt on my life at the Crossed Hands and the warning which somebody slipped into my pocket at the inquest show that they're afraid of what I might find out.' Lowe found his pipe and began stuffing tobacco into the bowl from his pouch. 'Both those moves were foolish, because it shows that somebody is afraid.'

'I suppose you haven't any suspicions as to who put that envelope in your pocket, sir?' said Hartley.

Lowe shook his head.

'Not the slightest,' he declared. 'It might have been one of half a dozen people. The only thing we do know is that it was somebody local. There were no strangers at the inquest.'

'Well, I'd give a lot to know what's really at the back of it all,' said Hartley fervently.

'Not more than I would,' answered Lowe. 'And we shall eventually if we wait long enough. These people will make a false move if we give them enough rope. They're already afraid, and that's a great point in our favour. If they'd leave well alone now they'd be safe, but I don't think they will. They'll try and consolidate their position, and that's where they're going to give themselves away. More criminals have been caught because they've been too anxious to cover up their tracks than by any other means. And I'm inclined to think that the same thing will happen in this case.'

'I hope you're right, sir,' said Hartley, and shortly afterwards took his leave.

Trevor Lowe spent the rest of the morning strolling about the grounds of Greytower, smoking and thinking.

So far as he was able he tried to put his fears regarding Arnold White out of his mind, and he found it very difficult. For his anxiety concerning his secretary's fate was very acute, and he found it constantly thrusting its head up to the exclusion of everything else.

Since the house was still servantless, he and Jim and McWraith had to get their own lunch, which they did with the aid of fresh supplies procured by McWraith from the village.

Jim had, however, learned that there was a servants' agency at Hythe, and during the meal he announced his intention of driving over during the afternoon and seeing what he could find.

'If I can't get hold of anybody,' he said, 'we shall have to shut the place up for the time being and stay at the hotel at Hythe.'

'Then I hope you find somebody,' mumbled McWraith, his mouth full of mutton chop. 'It would be a pity to leave here and chance missing whatever excitement may be going.'

They had washed up the things and Jim was setting out to fetch the car when the telephone bell rang.

McWraith answered it and called to Lowe.

'It's your boy friend, the superintendent,' he said as the dramatist took the receiver from his hand.

Hartley had news. He had just received

a telephone call from the Yard to say that Detective Inspector Shadgold and Detective Inspector Murley were coming down to see him and expected to arrive about four o'clock. It was in connection with Johnny Calling, and very important. He thought, perhaps, Lowe would like to be there.

'I should very much, Hartley,' answered the dramatist. 'Thanks for letting me know.'

He hung up the receiver and turned to McWraith.

'I wonder if you two would take me with you into Hythe,' he said.

'Of course,' answered the huge Scotsman promptly. 'It'll be a tight fit though.'

'I can manage to squeeze into the dickey-seat,' said Lowe. 'I shall probably be able to come back in my own car. I should think they've put the new tyres on by now.'

The hoot of a horn from outside warned them that Jim was waiting and impatient, and they joined him.

Lowe explained his altered plans — for he had at first arranged to stay behind

— and when McWraith had with difficulty packed himself in beside Jim he took his place in the rear seat.

They reached Hythe a little after three, and leaving Jim and McWraith to set out on their servant-hunting errand, Lowe entered the police station.

He found Hartley in his microscopic office at the back of the charge-room and sat down in the chair which the superintendent indicated.

'I phoned you, Mr. Lowe,' said Hartley, removing a pair of large horn-rimmed spectacles and carefully putting them away in a case, 'because it seemed to me that this visit might have some important bearing on this affair at Stonehurst. There must be something behind this Johnny Calling murder that the Yard know about for them to send down like this.'

'I agree with you,' said Lowe. 'Maybe they'll be able to give us just the line we're seeking.'

'That's what I'm hoping, sir,' said Hartley, nodding. 'The chief constable was on the phone just before the message came through from the Yard, wanting to know if I'd made any further discoveries. And when I told him I hadn't he suggested it would be a good plan to invite the help of Scotland Yard.'

He looked across at Lowe and pursed his lips.

'Well, naturally I don't want to do that if I can help it, Mr. Lowe. It would be a feather in my cap if I could pull this business off on my own — with your help, of course,' he added.

'Yes, I understand how you feel about it. It's a question of personal pride, isn't it?'

'You've hit it, sir,' answered Hartley, smiling. 'That's what it is. You see, this is the first big thing I've had the chance of handling, and I'd like to go through with it to the end.'

'Well, you know that it was more or less at the request of Inspector Shadgold that I came here,' said Lowe. 'That is, originally I was coming down, anyway, the next day. It was Johnny Calling's phone call that brought me before I intended. So, as far as the missing men are concerned, it's Shadgold's job, but these murders are, of course, in a different category. They happened in your district, and unless you call on the Yard for help they've no power to interfere. That's really what you're getting at in a roundabout way, isn't it?'

The superintendent's big face reddened.

'Yes, sir, that's it,' he said slowly. 'I was rather afraid these fellows who are coming down might — well, sort of take charge and persuade the chief constable to officially apply for help . . . '

'I don't know Murley,' interrupted Lowe, 'but so far as Shadgold is concerned you needn't worry. He's one of the best of good fellows, and he wouldn't dream of robbing you of any kudos — '

'Any what, sir?' asked the puzzled Hartley.

'Any credit,' supplemented Lowe. 'Besides which, while they're in this district you are their superior officer.'

'Yes, sir, I know that,' said Hartley. 'But I'm only a local man, and they're Yard men. Superior officer or not it makes a difference. However, I'm glad I mentioned it, sir.'

He began to talk about the arrangements that had been made for the inquest on the Norths for the following morning, and was still so engaged when a constable, looking rather flustered and nervous, announced the arrival of 'Detective Inspector Shadgold and Detective Inspector Murley.'

'Ask them to come in here, Tillet,' said Hartley, breaking off hastily in the middle of a sentence; and a second later the two Yard men were ushered into the office.

'Good afternoon, Superintendent,' began Murley; and then Shadgold who was behind him caught sight of Lowe.

'Hullo, Mr. Lowe!' he exclaimed. 'I knew you were down here somewhere, but I didn't expect to see you here.'

'I've come to hear what you've got to tell us concerning Johnny Calling,' said the dramatist, smiling.

'What do you know about Johnny Calling?' he asked quickly.

Shadgold looked at him suspiciously.

'Nothing at present — except that he was a burglar and that he's dead,' answered Lowe. 'But I shall be very interested to hear more.'

'I thought you'd already heard something,' grunted Shadgold, and when the dramatist shook his head: 'Well, then, I think Murley and I can supply you with some very interesting information.'

20

The Man in the Porch

'And that's why, immediately we learned about the identity of the dead man, we came down,' said Inspector Murley at the end of an hour. 'When Shadgold told me, I thought it was a clue that ought to be followed up at once.'

'You see, Mr. Lowe,' cut in Shadgold, 'it struck me that this drug ramp, 'slush' money and burglary epidemics were connected with this other business of the disappearances.'

'I think you're right,' said Lowe. 'Don't you, Hartley?'

The big superintendent nodded.

'I do,' he declared without hesitation. 'I think it's just the thing we've been looking for, sir. A line to the motive behind all these crimes.'

'It seems to me, sir,' said Murley, his thin, alert face alive with interest, 'that

Stonehurst is the headquarters of this gang.'

'I'm almost certain of that,' agreed Lowe. 'I'm beginning to understand now why those extraordinary changes took place two years ago, Hartley.'

'What changes were those?' asked Shadgold quickly.

'I think Superintendent Hartley had better tell you that,' answered the dramatist, and Hartley complied.

The two Scotland Yard men listened with interest, and when he had finished Murley whistled softly.

'I'd like to have a look at some of these newcomers,' he remarked. 'I've an idea that they might prove to be old friends.'

'We shall have to go carefully over that,' said Shadgold. 'If they're crooks, as we believe, we don't want to scare them. It would be easy to catch one or two, but the others would be off like the wind at the first sign of danger. We might as well pull in the lot while we're about it.'

Murley nodded.

'I agree,' he said heartily. 'The difficulty is to know who is in this business and who isn't. Some of these people who have come to live in the village may be quite innocent, and we don't want any trouble. Again, there may be some who have never passed through our hands, who are in it up to their necks, but whom we shouldn't recognise.'

'Yes, and they would get away if you acted precipitately,' answered the dramatist. 'And there wouldn't be a shred of evidence to convict them.'

'That's quite right, sir,' said Superintendent Hartley. 'It's going to be a tricky business, because, for one thing, all we've got to work on is conjecture. We've got no definite case against anybody. And for another, after these murders you can bet your life that these birds are going to be extra cautious. They know that the place is being watched by the police and they're not going to be so silly as to make any move that's likely to give them away.'

There was a short silence, broken by Lowe.

'Have you photographs of these men Freeman and Kenner?' he asked.

'Yes,' said Murley.

'Then,' went on the dramatist, 'I think it would be a good plan if you could get them down here and let Hartley have them. He's seen most of the people in the village and he might be able to identify them.'

'I'll have them sent down at once.' Murley looked across at Hartley. 'Can I use your 'phone, Super?'

'Of course.' Hartley pushed the instrument towards him, sliding it along the desk.

The inspector asked for 'Trunks,' and a few seconds later was speaking to Chief Inspector Watling at the Yard.

'They're being sent right away,' he said presently, hanging up the receiver.

'You see,' said Lowe, 'if we're lucky enough to narrow this down to one — or perhaps two — people whom we know are involved, we can keep a watch on their movements. And so long as they don't know we're watching them they'll lead us to the rest.'

'In that case I think it'd be just as well if Murley and I stayed for a while,' said Shadgold. 'Don't you?'

Lowe looked at Hartley.

Remembering their conversation prior to the arrival of the others, he wondered how the superintendent would take this suggestion. As he had rather expected, Hartley looked a little glum.

'Well — ' he began, and Lowe broke in before he could say any more.

'I think the superintendent would welcome your co-operation,' he said tactfully, 'if it was understood that so far as these murders are concerned your help would be more or less unofficial.'

'Of course, in that respect it would be,' said Shadgold quickly. 'That's entirely up to Superintendent Hartley. We haven't been asked to help. All we are officially interested in is the mystery surrounding the disappearances and the truth concerning this criminal gang, if it exists.'

Hartley's face cleared.

'In that case I'll be very grateful if you'll give me a hand,' he said.

'If you've decided to stay,' said the dramatist, 'why not come back and put up at Greytower? I'm sure Mr. Winslow will be only too glad, and you'll be right in the thick of it.'

'That's a very good idea, Mr. Lowe,' said Murley, 'only we shall have to be careful that we're not spotted.'

'There's no reason why you should be,' answered Lowe. 'It'll be dark before we get back, and you can keep well under cover during the day.'

As the two Yard men approved of the plan it was agreed that Lowe should put it up to Jim when he and McWraith returned from the servants' registry.

'If this criminal organisation exists,' said Lowe, when this had been settled, 'as I for one think it does, after what you've told me, they couldn't have chosen a better place than Stonehurst for their headquarters. A typical old English village is the last place one would think of looking for anything of the sort, and for one part of their operations the sea is most conveniently close.'

'You mean the drugs?' said Shadgold, and Lowe nodded.

'Exactly,' he replied. 'They could land any number of secret cargoes down by the coast with very little risk of detection.

And as for the rest of their activities' — he shrugged his shoulders — 'well, they could be carried on in comfort.'

'They won't be so comfortable if I can get my hands on 'em!' grunted Murley. 'I've had a pretty fair sickener of this job during the last eighteen months, working night and day with no results to show for it.'

'The person we want to lay our hands on is the man or woman at the back of it,' said Lowe.

'You agree with the Chief Commissioner, then, sir?' asked Murley.

'Most certainly I do,' declared the dramatist. 'Unusual as it is outside fiction to find a master-mind at work, I think we can safely assume that it is so in this case. From what you tell me, all these crimes have been most carefully planned. The distribution of the drugs and the bad notes, for instance. All that indicates a clever brain directing. And then supposing — as we are certain they are — that these disappearances are traceable to the same cause. Look at the clever way they have been carried out. These four Yard men have vanished without a trace, and that's not so easy as it sounds. Oh! yes, there's somebody directing operations, somebody responsible for the whole scheme — somebody who conceived the idea of turning a peaceful country village into a crooks' colony.'

'And it may be anybody,' put in Hartley gloomily. 'All the people that might have been able to tell us anything have been wiped out.'

'Including Mrs. North,' said Lowe quietly.

'She wiped herself out,' said the superintendent, and then, catching the expression on the dramatist's face, he added quickly: 'Don't you think so, sir?'

'It certainly looked like it,' admitted Lowe, 'but I must say I'm doubtful. It was such a very convenient thing for her to do.'

'Well, I don't see how she could have been murdered, and that's the only alternative,' protested Hartley. 'The door was locked when Dr. Grendon and I entered the room, and the windows were shut and fastened, and hadn't been tampered with. Nobody could have got at her.'

'There was one person who could,' said Lowe meaningly. 'Dr. Grendon.'

Hartley sat up in his chair with a jerk.

'Dr. Grendon?' he repeated incredulously. 'But he didn't go in on his own, sir. I was with him — '

'Not all the time you weren't,' broke in Lowe. 'He was alone with her when you came downstairs to us.'

'But,' exclaimed the superintendent, 'she was dead then — '

'How do you know she was dead then?' Lowe snapped out the question sharply, and as Hartley stared at him with dropped jaw, too surprised to reply, he went on quickly: 'Because Grendon told you so. But supposing at that time she wasn't dead, only sleeping? What was to prevent Grendon from killing her while they were left alone?'

'By Jove, Mr. Lowe,' interjected Shadgold. 'The man would have needed colossal nerve. Think of the risk.'

'It would have been a bigger risk to let her live if she knew as much as we think she knew,' retorted the dramatist.

There was a momentary hush of silence while the other three occupants of the tiny office stared at him.

'If this theory of yours is right,' said Hartley at last, 'I'd better arrange for an autopsy.'

'I think you ought to,' answered Lowe. 'Only it will have to be carried out secretly. It mustn't leak out that we suspect anything but accidental death or suicide, otherwise we shall put Grendon on his guard.'

'I'll see Dr. Peters and explain matters to him, sir,' said the superintendent.

'You're sure he's to be trusted?' warned Lowe. 'We can't be too careful.'

Hartley gave a confident smile.

'Oh, yes, sir,' he answered reassuringly, 'he can be trusted all right.'

'Well, if it should be proved that the woman was killed as you suggest, Mr. Lowe,' put in Shadgold, 'it will give us one of the people concerned in this business for certain.'

'And through him the whole bunch, I hope,' answered Lowe grimly. 'I've got an extraordinary incentive to run these people to earth, Shadgold — ' He stopped suddenly, and the inspector who knew that he was referring to Arnold White nodded sympathetically.

'Let's hope that no serious harm has come to Mr. White,' he said.

'There's just one reason why we can hope that,' answered the dramatist. 'It's a very faint one, but it's possible they may be keeping him alive to use as a hostage in case of emergency.'

He saw by their faces that none of them thought this was very likely, and, indeed, he had very little faith in the suggestion himself. But it was a forlorn hope, and he clung to it.

The constable came in at that moment to say that Jim Winslow was waiting outside, and Lowe went out to him, accompanied by Shadgold and Murley.

'The more the merrier,' said Jim when the dramatist had introduced the Scotland Yard men and had suggested that they should put up at Greytower. 'I've found a couple of good servants, an ex-serviceman and his wife, and they're coming over in the morning. So after to-night we shall have somebody to look after us.'

'In the meantime,' grinned McWraith, indicating a large package that rested precariously on his knees, 'We've got enough tinned food for a regiment.'

'I've no doubt that Shadgold and Inspector Murley will be glad to sample it,' remarked the dramatist. 'I'll just slip round to the garage and see if my car is ready, and then we can get along.'

'We'll go on ahead,' said Jim. 'You'll probably catch us up half-way.'

He drove off with a wave of his hand, and Lowe, Shadgold and Murley walked round to the garage.

The car was ready, and with the two Yard men in the back, Lowe brought it round to the police station, where they stopped for a moment to say good-bye to Hartley.

Just as they were leaving the constable came down the steps and thrust three blue papers into Lowe's hand.

'The subpoenas for the inquest, sir,' he explained. 'Will you give the other two to

Mr. Winslow and Mr. McWraith?'

Lowe promised, and they drove away.

He let the big Rolls out when they had negotiated the narrow streets of Hythe and, as Jim had predicted, caught up the other car four miles outside Stonehurst.

He passed it with a warning note from the klaxon, and then slowed so as to keep a uniform distance between them.

Turning it at the drive gate, he decreased the speed still more, and as he did so he heard above the almost imperceptible purr of the engine the sound of running, stumbling feet.

They came from the direction of the house and seemed to be going away from him.

He opened his lips to remark on this to Shadgold and Murley, but before he could frame the words there came from out of the darkness ahead a shrill scream.

'My God! What was that?' exclaimed Shadgold leaning forward. 'Did you hear it?'

'I heard it,' snapped Lowe, and pressing his foot on the accelerator, sent the great car bounding forward.

He swung round the bend in the drive, brushing the shrubbery at the side, and then, as the glare of the headlights fell full on the door of the house, he uttered an exclamation.

'Look there!' he shouted, but Shadgold and Murley had already seen.

In the white light of the car's lamps two men were struggling frantically, while a third was running towards them.

Again came that hoarse scream of fear and terror, but this time it ceased abruptly and ended in a choking, throaty little gulp.

One of the desperately fighting men crumpled up and fell limply across the bottom step of the flight that led up to the porch.

Lowe brought the car to a jarring halt, and as he sprang out the two other men wheeled and dashed away into the darkness beyond the range of the light.

'Go after those two, Shadgold!' cried the dramatist over his shoulder as he ran towards the figure on the step. 'I think there's been murder done.'

The Scotland Yard man went racing

away in pursuit and, reaching the steps, Lowe bent over the sprawling man.

He was lying face downwards as he had fallen, and already the white stone was red with the blood that welled from under his body.

Gently Lowe turned him over and saw the knife that was buried to the hilt in his throat.

A glance showed him that the man was dead, and also that he was the Frenchman, Mr. Lucia, the tenant of the Martins' cottage!

21

At the Martins' Cottage

He was still stooping over the body when Jim and McWraith joined him.

'Is he dead?' asked Jim breathlessly, staring down at the motionless form, and Lowe nodded.

'Yes,' he answered. 'One of you had better phone Hythe and tell Hartley.'

'I will,' said Jim, and running up the steps he fumbled for his key.

He found it and opened the front door.

'What in the world were those men doing here?' asked McWraith, his usually healthy face an unpleasant grey. 'There were three of them, weren't there?'

Again Lowe nodded.

'Shadgold and Murley have gone after the other two,' he said. 'They ran away towards the back of the house. I — '

He broke off as there came the sound of two shots some distance away, fired in rapid succession.

'Good God!' muttered McWraith. 'They ought to advertise this place as 'Stonehurst for excitement!''

'It's too exciting,' said Lowe. 'I hope those shots came from Shadgold and Murley and not from the other men, or we may have some more excitement.'

He knelt down and began to search the pockets of the dead man, laying the contents neatly on the step.

There were not many. A wallet containing a few notes; a letter; a few shillings and some coppers in change; a watch and chain, and a bunch of keys were all he found.

He stared at the meagre collection with knitted brow. Why had this man been killed on the threshold of Greytower? Had he been on his way to the house when he had been set upon?

Remembering those running, stumbling steps, it certainly looked like it.

Lowe tried to reconstruct in his imagination what had happened.

Lucia must have been walking up the drive, when he became aware that he was being followed, and ran for sanctuary where there was none to offer him.

He probably had not known that the house was empty. But why had he come at all? Had he, too, been in possession of some knowledge regarding Stonehurst's secret that he was anxious to impart?

While Lowe was still thinking Jim came out of the door.

'Hartley's coming over at once,' he said in a low voice. 'He was terribly shocked at the news.'

'I'm not surprised,' muttered Lowe; 'this village of yours seems full of battle, murder and sudden death.'

Jim came down the steps and stood beside him.

'Do you think he was coming here to see us?' he asked.

'It looks like it,' replied Lowe.

He rose to his feet and mechanically brushed the knees of his trousers.

'We'd better leave him here until Hartley and the doctor have seen him.'

He picked up the wallet and went carefully through it in the hope of finding something that he'd overlooked in his previous hasty search.

But there was nothing. The letter was no help at all. It was merely a bill from the local newsagent.

He was returning it to its envelope when Shadgold arrived panting and exhausted.

'They got away,' he said jerkily. 'We lost them in a wood over there behind the house.'

'Who fired the shots?' asked Lowe.

'They did,' said the burly inspector; 'and they hit Murley too.'

'It's nothing much,' said Murley, coming up a little shakily. 'A bullet slashed my wrist.'

He held out a hand dripping with blood.

'You'd better let me tie that up,' said McWraith. 'I'm very good at first-aid.'

He took Murley by the arm and led him into the house and Shadgold turned to Lowe.

'Who is he?' he asked, pointing to the dead man.

'A Frenchman called Lucia,' answered the dramatist. 'I've told you about him.'

'I remember.' The Scotland Yard man nodded and rubbed his head. 'I wonder what he was doing here and why they killed him?'

Lowe explained the conclusion he had come to, and Shadgold agreed with him.

'I expect you're right, Mr. Lowe,' he said. 'Poor devil! There's something horrible in the thought of his running for help to an empty house. Did you find anything in his pockets that is likely to help?'

The dramatist shook his head.

'Nothing,' he replied. 'That's all there was; you can see for yourself.'

Shadgold looked hastily over the small heap.

'Nothing here,' he grunted. 'Maybe we shall find something among his things at the cottage.'

'I hope we may,' said Lowe. 'We'll go along there as soon as Hartley arrives.'

The superintendent arrived in an ambulance a quarter of an hour later, a perplexed and worried man, bringing with him Dr. Peters.

'Well, well,' said the police doctor, his

scraggy neck longer than ever. 'Another, eh? This is getting monotonous, you know! And I used to say that Stonehurst was a dead and alive hole. If this sort of thing goes on much longer it'll be completely dead!'

'How did it happen, sir?' asked Hartley, and Lowe told him.

'You weren't able to recognise either of the men?' said the superintendent gloomily.

'No,' said Lowe. 'All I can tell you about them is they were of medium height and wore overcoats and caps.'

'Well, it doesn't require a great deal of medical knowledge to see how he died,' broke in Dr. Peters, looking up from his position beside the body. 'The knife severed the jugular and windpipe. It must have been driven with considerable force, and, of course, death would have been almost instantaneous.'

He straightened up and, feeling in his pocket, produced a cigarette-case.

'You can take him away now, if you want to.'

'I'll have the knife first,' said Hartley.

'There may be prints on that hilt.'

He took out his handkerchief, wrapped it round the handle, and withdrew the weapon from the wound.

'Did you notice whether the man who killed him was wearing gloves?' He addressed the question to both Lowe and Shadgold, but it was the dramatist who answered.

'I couldn't be sure, but I don't think he was,' he said.

'I didn't notice,' confessed Shadgold. 'The whole thing happened so quickly.'

'I'll have it dusted anyhow,' grunted Hartley.

He put the knife, still wrapped in the handkerchief, carefully away in his pocket and called to the constable who was standing near.

As the man came over Lowe whispered something in the superintendent's ear.

'All right, sir,' Hartley nodded. 'I'll finish here, and then I'll join you.'

'Come on, Shadgold,' said Lowe; 'we'll go down to the cottage where this fellow was staying and see if we can find anything there.'

'I'll drive you,' said Jim, who had been near enough to hear what was said. 'I know where the place is.'

'Fine!' agreed Lowe, and followed him past his own car to where Jim had left the other.

They had to back past the ambulance and down the drive, for there was no room for them to turn, but Jim managed it without mishap, and once they reached the road, it only took a few minutes to the Martins' cottage.

It was a pretty little place, with a thatched roof, standing in a narrow lane that opened on to The Green.

They left the car at the end of the lane and reaching the cottage, found that it was in complete darkness.

As they walked up the stone paved path Lowe took from his pocket the bunch of keys belonging to the dead man, which he had brought with him.

'I don't know which of these — ' he was beginning, and then as they reached the porch he saw that the door was half-open.

Unless Lucia had left it like that, which

was unlikely, somebody had been there before them — might even be there still — and, with a whispered warning to Shadgold and Jim, Lowe craned forward and listened.

There was no sound from the darkness within, but that was no proof that the place was empty. They had made no secret of their approach, and if there was somebody lurking inside they would have been heard.

Lowe pushed the door farther open and cautiously stepped across the threshold.

Again he listened, but still there was no sound. Slipping his hand into his pocket, he took out his torch and flashed the light into the hall.

It was empty.

Turning the ray on to the lock of the door, he saw that the wood round it was splintered and the catch into which the bolt shot wrenched from its fastening.

'Somebody has broken in here recently,' he whispered. 'But I think they must have gone. Shall we risk it?'

Shadgold nodded.

'Come on then,' said the dramatist, and stepped into the hall.

Crack!

A bullet whistled past his head and splintered the edge of the door. He hastily switched out his light.

Crack! Crack!

Two more shots followed so closely that the reports sounded almost like one.

He saw the spears of orange flame from the stairway and pulled Shadgold and Jim down with him as he dropped flat.

A fusillade of bullets whined angrily over their heads, and then came a rush of feet as somebody charged towards them.

Lowe caught sight of a man's figure and, shooting out his hand, gripped an ankle. There was a smothered oath and the thud of a falling body.

'Hang on to him!' exclaimed the dramatist, and switched on his torch again.

But the man was already up and running down the path.

Jim, who had managed to regain his feet, gave chase and overtook the fugitive at the gate, but with a snarl of rage the man turned and caught him a stinging blow on the point of the chin.

An inch to the right and it would have been a knock-out. As it was it sent Jim staggering backwards into a clump of laurel.

'That,' said Trevor Lowe, as he scrambled to his feet, 'was a near thing!'

He took off his hat and pointed silently to two neat holes that had been drilled through the crown!

22

Mr. Lucia — from Paris

'He must have come straight on here after Lucia was killed,' said Lowe, putting his hat back on his head, 'and our arrival disturbed him.'

He walked into the hall, flashing his light around. The place was very plainly furnished, in rather an old-fashioned way, and on the carpet by the narrow staircase he found the marks of muddy feet.

'When he heard us coming he hid by the curve of the staircase, hoping to take us by surprise.'

'Which he succeeded in doing,' grunted Shadgold.

'He had a punch like the kick of an ox,' said Jim, tenderly caressing his bruised jaw. 'I wish I'd been able to hold him.'

'I wish you had,' said Lowe. 'I'd have liked to have had a few words with him. Now we're here we may as well have a look round, though I'm afraid we're too late to find anything.'

He opened a door to the left of the hall, and found himself in a small sitting-room.

It was fairly comfortably furnished, and on the centre table was an oil-lamp. He lit this and glanced quickly about.

'You see,' he muttered, and Shadgold nodded.

The room had been thoroughly ransacked.

There was a small bookcase containing for the most part old and out-of-date novels, pamphlets and old magazines, and some of these had been pulled out and thrown on to the floor.

An old-fashioned bureau standing against one wall had been broken open and most of its contents scattered in all directions.

A cupboard by the side of the fireplace was open, the broken door hanging half off its hinges.

'I wonder what he was looking for,' said Shadgold, gazing round at the wreckage.

'What we came to look for,' replied Lowe. 'Anything the dead man may have left behind that would give these people away.'

'Do you think Lucia was a member of the gang?' asked the Scotland Yard man.

'I should say it was probable,' answered the dramatist, biting his lip.

'And he tried to double-cross them, eh?' continued Shadgold. 'He was going to spill the beans when they got him?'

'That seems the most probable explanation,' replied Lowe. 'He fell out with his associates over something or other and, knowing that I was staying at Greytower, came round to see me. What do you think?'

'It's a likely theory, anyway,' agreed the inspector.

He went over and began poking among the litter in the bureau.

'I suppose we may as well make a search, in case that fellow overlooked something.'

'Yes, there's just a faint chance we might find something,' said Lowe. 'If you take the bureau I'll deal with these books.'

They searched diligently while Jim stood by the door and looked on, but they found nothing.

The papers in the bureau mostly

belonged to the original owner of the cottage, and consisted of letters and receipted bills.

There were one or two unpaid bills addressed to Mr. Lucia, but nothing else.

Neither was there anything among the books.

In the fireplace, however, Lowe found a heap of charred paper, and going over it, carefully extracted a thicker wad from underneath the rest.

'This looks like a book of some description,' he said, bringing it under the light. 'Part of the leather cover is still unburned.'

He spread a sheet of paper on the table and, laying the charred mass on it, examined it carefully.

'Yes, look here.' He glanced up at Shadgold, who was peering over his shoulder. 'You can just see a 'D' and part of an 'I.' It was a diary.'

'Is there anything left of it that's readable?' asked Shadgold eagerly.

Lowe shook his head.

'No, unfortunately,' he replied. 'This looks as if it was only the cover. I think the pages were torn out and burned separately.'

He straightened up, shot a quick frowning glance round.

'There's nothing more here,' he said. 'Let's see if the rest of the cottage will prove luckier.'

He took the lamp and, followed by Shadgold and Jim, explored the lower floor.

The sitting-room with the kitchen and scullery comprised the whole of this, and there was nothing at all in the kitchen and scullery except some dirty dishes in the sink and a few articles of food.

They opened all the cupboards and searched through their miscellaneous contents, which were mostly rubbish, but their diligence went unrewarded.

'There's only upstairs now,' said Lowe. 'Come on, we'll see what we can find there.'

There were two rooms upstairs, a large room over the sitting-room and hall, and a smaller one over the kitchen.

This was locked, but the key was in the door, and Lowe turned it and looked in.

Apparently it had not been used by Lucia, for the bed was bare; the sheets and blankets neatly folded and lying near the footboard.

Apart from the bed there was only a washstand, a kitchen chair, and a narrow wardrobe.

Lowe opened the wardrobe and found that it was empty except for three coat-hangers and the lid of a cardboard box.

The drawer in the lower part was also empty.

'Nothing here,' he muttered. 'I don't think Lucia used the room at all.'

They came out, shut the door, and went into the larger room.

This was better furnished. The bed was a double one, and beside the washstand and wardrobe there was a dressing-table and a chest of drawers.

The place was tidy; the dead man's brushes, combs and collar-box were neatly arranged on the top of the chest of drawers; his studs and links filled a little glass tray on the dressing-table.

There was no sign of confusion, and Lowe's eyes sparkled.

'I think we interrupted the intruder before he got as far as this,' he said. 'Probably he was just on his way upstairs when we came.'

He set the lamp down on the top of the chest of drawers and pulled open the wardrobe.

There were two suits of clothes carefully hung up on hangers and three pairs of shoes complete with trees.

He went through the pockets, but they were empty.

'You try those drawers, Shadgold, while I look through the dressing-table,' he said, nodding towards the chest; and the Scotland Yard man went over to it.

There was very little in the dressing-table — a few ties and handkerchiefs in the right-hand drawer, and nothing at all in the left.

'Any luck?' he asked.

'Nothing but shirts and underclothes,' grunted the inspector disgustedly. 'Not a scrap of paper anywhere.'

Lowe frowned and rubbed his chin.

'Well, there's nowhere else to look,' he said irritably.

'Afraid there isn't.' Shadgold closed the last drawer with a vicious bang.

'Wait a minute, though,' said the dramatist. 'What about his luggage? He must have brought his things here in something. Suitcases or a trunk.'

He went quickly over to the bed and lifted the valence.

'Yes, here we are,' he said triumphantly. 'What a fool I was not to have thought of this at once.'

He stooped and dragged out a cabin-trunk.

It was an ancient battered affair, and when he tried to open it he found it was securely locked.

Pulling out Lucia's bunch of keys, he tried three that looked as if they might fit, and the third one did.

Raising the lid, he peered inside and gave an exclamation of satisfaction.

'This may give us something,' he said. 'Look here!'

They looked and saw that the trunk was half-full of papers and letters.

Lowe picked up one of the letters and glanced at the address, and as he did so his lips formed into a silent whistle.

'So that's who Mr. Lucia of Paris was,' he said softly, and handed the envelope to Shadgold.

The inspector took it, and as he read the name and address the surprise on his face was almost ludicrous.

'Good God!' he ejaculated. 'And we thought he was a crook!'

The envelope was addressed to:

'MONSIEUR HENRI DUPIN,
DIRECTION DE LA SÛRETÉ GÉNÉRALE,
PARIS.'

23

Surprise

There was no doubt that the dead man's real name had been Henri Dupin, and less that he had been an officer of the special branch of the French Sûreté.

At the bottom of the trunk Lowe found his passport and papers of identification, which proved this apart from anything else.

He had just finished glancing through these when Superintendent Hartley arrived and the discovery was made known to him.

He was justifiably astonished.

'What was he doing in Stonehurst?' he said. 'Do you think he can have been here on the same job as we are?'

'There's not the slightest doubt he was,' answered Lowe. 'But we may be able to make definitely certain when we've been through these letters. They appear to be answers to reports and further instructions, and have apparently been sent on to him from London under a covering envelope. There is no Stonehurst postmark on any of them. I suggest that we take this trunk as it stands back to the house and go through the contents at our leisure.'

Hartley agreed, and between them they carried the trunk down the stairs and out to the waiting car.

Except for the bloodstain on the step there was no sign of the tragedy when they arrived at the house, and they found Ian McWraith and Inspector Murley — the latter's wrist neatly bandaged — sitting before the fire in the drawing-room.

While Shadgold hastily explained to Murley what had happened Jim and Hartley brought in the trunk and helped Lowe transfer its contents to the table.

Drawing up a chair, the dramatist began to sort the papers and letters, and spent the next hour going carefully through them.

They were all in French, and when he

had read them he found that he was just a little nearer the solution of the mystery.

One document in particular was most illuminating, for it consisted of a rough draft of what was evidently the report prepared by Dupin for his superiors in Paris.

Lowe passed on his discoveries to his interested and impatient audience.

'It seems,' he said, 'that the man was here primarily to investigate the drug business. There are letters here from the Prefecture of Police that prove that conclusively. It had apparently come to their notice some months ago that cocaine, heroin, opium and other drugs were being smuggled from Germany and Belgium through France, and then going to some unknown destination in England. How Dupin discovered or suspected that that destination was Stonehurst there is no record, but in this draft report he mentions a ship at anchor two miles out at sea, which he has seen on several occasions and always at night. He also mentions something about 'nine,' though whether this refers to a time or a number there is nothing to show. The draft is very sketchy; more a collection of disjointed notes than anything else.'

'Anyway,' remarked Shadgold, 'it proves that we were right. Stonehurst is the headquarters of this bunch of crooks.'

Lowe nodded.

'Oh, yes, it proves that,' he answered, 'but unfortunately it doesn't mention any names.'

'It's a great pity that that diary was destroyed, sir,' said Superintendent Hartley. 'It possibly contained a lot more information.'

'It *is* a pity,' said the dramatist, 'but it can't be helped. We can only be thankful that we arrived in time to prevent these papers being destroyed too.'

'I wonder why this fellow didn't enlist the help of the Yard,' muttered Murley. 'It seems funny, don't you think so?'

'There's a letter here from the Sûreté suggesting that he should,' replied Lowe. 'Why he didn't, of course, I don't know, but I should imagine he was trying to collect something more definite before doing so.'

'Well, sir, the thing that seems most vital at the moment,' said Superintendent Hartley, 'is what line of action are we going to take?'

'We could get in touch with the Sûreté,' grunted Shadgold, 'and find out what they can tell us. But apart from that we're no better off than we were before. Short of arresting everybody in the village I don't see what we can do.'

'It *is* a little difficult,' admitted Lowe, frowning.

'A little difficult!' Shadgold snorted, and thrust his hands deep into the pockets of his trousers. 'It's impossible! We've no real evidence against a single soul.'

'What we've got to do is to find some,' said Lowe cheerfully. 'I suggest that careful inquiries should be made about all these fresh inhabitants. We're almost bound to come upon something. Remember, these people are not amateurs, they're professional crooks, and they've got a past. The thing to do is to find out all about them. Who they are and where they came from.'

'That shouldn't be difficult,' said Murley.

'It shouldn't,' agreed the dramatist, 'providing we're allowed to do it.'

Something in the tone of his voice made Shadgold look at him quickly.

'What exactly do you mean by that?' he asked.

Lowe rose to his feet and crossed over to the fireplace. With his back to the fire he looked from one to the other for a moment in silence.

'I'll tell you what I mean,' he said at last seriously. 'I think we're all of us in considerable danger. At the present moment we're the only persons who know anything definite about this criminal organisation which is dangerous to their safety. Scotland Yard is aware of the existence of such a gang, or rather suspects that it exists. The French police are in a similar position, but we have more knowledge than anybody. We know that this gang consists of the residents of Stonehurst or some of them. We don't know who, but we're getting sufficiently close to make them uneasy. And they know this. The person who controls them knows it. And they're not going to sit down quietly while we pursue our inquiries further.'

'What can they do?' demanded Shadgold.

Lowe shrugged his shoulders.

'What did they do in the case of Locker, Scory and the other men who stumbled on their secret?' he said grimly. 'What did they do when they found out that Calling, North and his wife were going to squeal? What have they done with Arnold White and, more recently, to Dupin — '

'But,' interrupted Shadgold, 'they can't do anything to us.' He look hastily round. 'There are six of us — '

'There are probably a great deal more of them,' said Lowe before he could complete his sentence. 'We don't know how many there are, but we do know they are desperate people who will stick at nothing to ensure their safety. And we represent the only immediate danger to that safety. I've no doubt that we're being watched, and that the man who escaped from that cottage has reported by now that he was interrupted before he had time to finish his job. They therefore don't know how much we may have discovered and what Dupin left behind, and if they have any sense they will do their utmost to prevent that knowledge leaving Stonehurst. So long as we are prevented from imparting what we know and suspect to anybody else they're comparatively safe.'

'Good heavens, sir!' ejaculated Superintendent Hartley. 'Are you seriously suggesting that some attempt will be made on us to-night?'

'I am!' declared the dramatist gravely. 'I've been trying to put myself in the place of these people and conjecturing what I should do under the same circumstances.'

'By Jove!' exclaimed McWraith. 'If you're right, it looks as though we're going to have a pleasant time.'

'I think you're rather exaggerating, Mr. Lowe,' said Inspector Murley, shaking his head. 'These people would never dare attempt anything against us. With the Frenchman it was different. He was only one man — '

'Supposing, though, that Mr. Lowe should be right,' put in Jim Winslow. 'Wouldn't it be a good plan for somebody to get on the phone to Scotland Yard and tell them exactly how the matter stands at present? That would be some sort of safeguard.'

'It's an excellent idea,' agreed the dramatist. 'Don't you think so, Shadgold?'

'I do,' grunted Shadgold, struggling to his feet. 'I'll go and do it now.'

He went out into the hall, and they heard him lift the receiver.

A minute later he was back again, his expression rather troubled.

'There's no answer from the Exchange,' he announced soberly. 'The line is dead.'

Hartley sprang up with a startled exclamation.

'You mean — ' he began and stopped.

'He means,' said Lowe quietly, 'that the line's been cut!'

'Then you were right,' muttered Jim.

'I'm afraid so,' said the dramatist. 'And

I think you would find, if you tried, that Stonehurst has been cut off from all telephonic and telegraphic communication with the rest of the world to-night!'

The words had scarcely left his lips when Shadgold, who had remained standing by the open door, suddenly swung round.

'Listen!' he said sharply.

They listened, startled by the suddenness of his ejaculation. At first they could hear nothing, and then they heard the sound that had attracted his attention — the sound of hurried running footsteps coming up the drive.

They were light steps and uneven, as though the runner was exhausted. They heard them patter up the stone steps leading to the front door and then there came an agitated knocking.

Shadgold made a half-turn towards the hall, but Lowe's voice stopped him.

'Be careful,' warned the dramatist; 'you don't know who it is.'

'It sounded like a woman,' grunted the inspector.

The agitated knocking was repeated, louder and more frenzied.

'Mr. Winslow!' came a faint voice. 'Mr. Winslow, let me in! For God's sake, let me in!'

'That's Miss Heyford's voice,' cried Jim, springing to his feet. 'We must let her in, Mr. Lowe. Something serious may have happened.'

He was across the room and at the hall door before he had finished speaking. Wrenching back the catch, he flung the door open, and Jill Heyford almost fell into his arms.

'Shut the door,' she said weakly. 'Shut the door! They're coming!'

Supporting her with an arm round her waist, Jim half-led, half-carried her into the drawing-room, and sat her down on an easy chair.

'Who are coming?' he demanded.

She tried to speak, but for a moment she was too breathless, and could only point shakily in the direction of the still open front door.

Lowe went out into the hall and shut it, taking the precaution to slip the bolt.

'That what you wanted?' he asked; and she nodded.

'Yes,' she panted huskily. 'Shut all the doors and the windows — '

'It will only be a waste of time,' said a harsh, metallic voice from the doorway. 'Put up your hands, please — everybody, or we'll drill you so full of holes you won't know where the draught's coming from!'

24

The Sentence

They had been so occupied with what the girl was saying that none had noticed that the hall and open doorway had become filled with men.

Now, as they swung quickly round at the sound of that harsh, grating voice, they could see them lined up behind the masked figure that had entered the room and was covering them with a heavy automatic held in one of his gloved hands.

The other men carried automatics too, the muzzles of which were all pointing steadily at the little group round Jill Heyford.

'Rather a surprise to you,' said the spokesman, his eyes above the handkerchief that was tied over nose and mouth moving restlessly from one to the other. 'The girl's warning came too late

— anyway, it would have been too late. We came in through the Tower. We had our own keys.'

'What do you want?' asked Lowe.

'What do we want?' mimicked the man with the automatic. 'What do you think we want? A friendly chat and a drink? Because if you do, you'd better think again. Keep your hands up!'

He swung the pistol towards McWraith with a snarl, as the big Scotsman's arms moved.

'What's the idea?' began Shadgold, his face purple with anger, but the other interrupted him.

'You'll know soon enough,' he snapped. 'At the moment keep quiet and do as you're told!'

Without turning his head he addressed the crowd of men behind him.

'Come and tie them up!' he ordered, 'and make a good job of it.'

Six of them stepped forward, dragging thin blindcord from their pockets as they did so.

Inspector Murley uttered an exclamation as one of these, a ferrety-faced little man with a broken nose, approached him.

'I know you,' he said. 'You're 'Sniffy' Smith. We wondered where you'd be hiding yourself.'

'You keep your mouth shut, Murley,' snarled the little man. 'You won't be wonderin' about anythin' long!'

'You will!' retorted Murley coolly. 'You'll be wondering why you were such a damned fool when you hear your sentence.'

'I won't be hearin' no sentence,' growled 'Sniffy' Smith. 'You can take that from me.'

'Don't talk,' said the man in the mask impatiently. 'Get on with what you've got to do.'

In fifteen minutes it was all over. Under the menacing muzzles of the automatics held by the remainder of the gang Lowe and the others were securely bound and reduced to helplessness.

They had to submit quietly, realising that in the circumstances it would have been suicidal to offer any resistance.

'That's right,' said the man approvingly when his orders had been carried out, and pocketed his pistol. 'You can put your guns away, boys.'

'You'll suffer a heavy penalty for this,' growled Superintendent Hartley, his voice hoarse with rage.

'I don't think so,' was the answer. 'In fact it is to avoid the possibility of suffering any penalty at all that I have taken this step.'

'What do you think you're going to do?' asked Lowe steadily. 'If you're thinking of murdering us as you did Dupin and the others, I assure you you won't get away with it. The police know we're here and — '

'Do you think I'm a child?' said the man in the mask contemptuously. 'You'll die, but nobody will know how you died. They won't know that you were deliberately killed. The whole world will sympathise with you over the terrible accident, though I'm afraid you will get neither satisfaction nor consolation from the fact.'

Lowe felt himself go rather cold at the malignancy in the man's voice. What horrible things had he in mind? What was this accident that he had planned?

Something of what he was thinking must have been expressed in his face, for the man went on quickly:

'I see that your curiosity has been aroused. I've no doubt that your companions are equally curious. That's only natural, so I'll tell you exactly what is going to happen to you all.' He seated himself on the arm of a chair and looked from one to the other.

If he expected them to say anything he was disappointed, for nobody spoke.

'When it first became clear to me that the only way to safeguard myself and my friends was to kill you,' he began calmly, 'I was faced with rather a problem. Ordinary murder was out of the question; enough of that had been done already, and any further crime would only have the effect of defeating my object. If six of you were found dead by unnatural means the whole of that very efficient organisation, Scotland Yard, would be put into operation to find out the reason. The result of that would undoubtedly mean disaster for us — I do not pretend that we can hope to fight the entire police force. But for several unfortunate incidents which could not be avoided, the searchlight of suspicion would never have been turned on Stonehurst at all — I read that phrase in a book somewhere, but it fits very well in this case. But now that it has been, the light has got to be turned out, and quickly. You people at the moment represent the light. With you silenced suspicion may remain for a little while, but providing we are careful and lie low, it will gradually die down. The murders that have already been committed will pass into the 'unsolved crimes' category, and everything will be, from our point of view, as it should be. To revert to the means by which I mean to dispose of you. If you think for a moment, I am sure you will realise that there is only one way by which your deaths could be achieved without it being obviously murder. Only one 'accident' that could logically account for six people being killed under one roof. That way is — fire.'

A little horrified exclamation came from the girl, and he looked towards her.

'That will not apply to you, Miss Heyford,' he said. 'When I was making my plans I had not reckoned on your appearance, and therefore some other way will be found to deal with you.'

'Good God!' cried Shadgold, his face white. 'Do you mean you're going to burn us to death? Set fire to the house while we're tied up like this — '

'Nearly right, but not quite,' broke in the masked man. 'I'm going to set fire to the house, yes, but none of you will be tied up when I do so. That would be foolish, since traces might be left for anybody who afterwards came to examine the scene of the holocaust. I have a better scheme than that. My friend, Dr. Grendon, has provided me with a drug which will render you unconscious until everything is over. After it has been administered the cords will be removed and everything will be left as natural as possible.'

They stared at him as he finished speaking, stunned with the appalling horror of the idea.

Murley was the first to find his voice.

'You don't think you can get away with it, do you?' he croaked hoarsely. 'Don't you see that the first thing that will be asked is why did six men sit quietly down and allow themselves to be burnt to death. If the house caught fire in a natural way we should know it soon enough for at least some of us to get away.'

'Besides,' said Superintendent Hartley, the sweat standing out in little beads on his large forehead, 'how do you intend to account for my presence? They'll be expecting me back at the police station at Hythe very shortly and — '

'I have thought of all the possibilities you mention,' interrupted the man in the mask, 'and I have taken the necessary precautions to overcome them. A telephone message was put through to Hythe a quarter of an hour ago, purporting to come from you, Superintendent, and stating that you were in the middle of a conference which would probably take a considerable time, and therefore you were staying the night. With regard to Inspector Murley's objections, the explanation is quite simple. The house will not be fired until one o'clock. At that hour, in the natural course of events, you would reasonably be expected to have gone to bed. That is exactly where you will be.'

Lowe passed the tip of his tongue over his lips, which were dry and hard.

The scheme was simple, and yet deadly efficient. If carried out according to plan there was every chance that it would be regarded as a tragic accident.

The nearest fire-station was at Hythe, and since he guessed that precautions had been taken to destroy any telephonic communications, the fire would have nearly burnt itself out before they could be notified and the first engine arrived.

The masked man rose to his feet and glanced at his watch.

'It is now,' he said, 'ten minutes to eleven. You have two hours and ten minutes to think about it. In the meantime there are certain preparations that have to be carried out. At half-past twelve we shall come back and administer the drug; until then you will be left alone. But I warn you that you can put all thoughts of escape out of your mind. The house is well guarded, with an armed man at every exit. So no one, even if they should get free, would be able to go very far. And this will also prevent any possible help from reaching you from outside.'

He walked over to the door, paused for a moment on the threshold to give a last look round, and went out, closing it behind him.

Lowe looked at the helpless figures of his companions. They had a little over an hour and a half to find some means of escape from the appalling fate that awaited them. Unless a miracle happened it looked impossible.

25

Ten Seconds

'We seem to be in a pretty nasty position, Mr. Lowe,' muttered Shadgold, breaking a short silence.

'Very nasty indeed,' agreed Lowe.

'Do you think there's any hope of help arriving from outside?' whispered Jim.

'Quite candidly, I don't,' answered the dramatist. 'The majority of the village is in bed and asleep. Apart from which, there's a guard around the house. Any stray help that might by a miracle arrive would soon be dealt with.'

'It looks as though we're for it,' grunted Inspector Murley. 'I'd like to have five minutes with that devil in the mask!'

'I'd like ten,' growled Shadgold. 'There's something funny about him. His voice sounds familiar, but I'm hanged if I can place it.'

'I thought that, too,' said Murley.

'Probably we've had him through our hands at some time or another. By Jove, he can talk, can't he? He likes to hear the sound of his own voice.'

The expression on Shadgold's face changed and he looked across at Trevor Lowe. Before he could say anything more, however, an exclamation from McWraith stopped him.

'I say,' he said suddenly, 'I believe I can get my hands free!'

While they had been talking he had been straining at the cords which bound his wrists, and his enormous strength had succeeded in stretching them until they were almost loose.

Lowe rolled over towards him.

'Try your best,' he urged. 'If you can get free you'll be able to release us.'

'A lot of good it'll do if he does,' grunted Shadgold. 'We couldn't get out of the house.'

'All the same, we wouldn't be helpless,' said Lowe. 'Go on, McWraith!'

The big Scotsman pulled and tugged, and then eventually succeeded in wrenching one hand free.

'Done it!' he panted, setting to work on the knots at his ankles.

Five minutes later he was scrambling to his feet with a broad grin.

'That's better,' he said. 'Now I'll have a shot at you.'

He came over to Lowe.

'There's a penknife in my waistcoat pocket,' said the dramatist. 'Use that. It'll be quicker.'

McWraith searched for it, found it, and opening it, slashed through the cords.

'Now it's your turn, Jim,' he said, and he had just succeeded in freeing his friend, when the door opened and 'Sniffy' Smith came in.

'The gov'nor thinks I'd better keep an eye on you — ' he began, and then as he saw that three of the prisoners were free, he gave a shout of alarm. ''Ere, what's up?' he cried, and his hand flew to his pocket, but McWraith in two bounds had reached him, and before he could reach the pistol a pair of huge arms were wrapped round him and he was borne struggling to the floor.

But his shout had been heard, for even

as Lowe and Jim made a dash to the door to shut it there came a rush of feet and the masked man, accompanied by four of the others, burst in.

'Look out!' he cried; 'some of them have got free.'

'Come on,' muttered Lowe in Jim's ear. 'Rush them and make for the Tower.'

His fist shot out as one of the men sprang at him and catching the fellow on the point of the jaw, sent him staggering back against the wall.

With Jim at his heels, Lowe whisked through the doorway and went racing along towards the kitchen.

'Catch them, you fool!' cried the masked man, 'but don't shoot if you can avoid it.'

The three men who were with him came pounding along after the fugitives, but Lowe and Jim had taken them so much by surprise that they had a good start.

They reached the kitchen a couple of yards in advance of their pursuers, and here disaster almost overtook them. The doorway was blocked by a pile of petrol cans, which they only saw when they had almost tumbled over them.

Without pausing, however, they succeeded in jumping the obstacle, and as they landed two men sprang up and tried to bar their path.

Jim accounted for one with a vicious swing which caught the man behind the ear, sending him sprawling with a squeak of pain.

The other leaped at Lowe and tried to grab him by the throat, but the dramatist ducked and butted him full in the stomach.

He collapsed with a grunt, falling with a loud clatter among the petrol cans.

'Come on!' panted Lowe, and ran for the door leading for the Tower.

It was open, and, racing down the narrow passage, they found themselves a few seconds later in the Tower room.

'Up the stairs!' jerked the dramatist breathlessly, dragging his torch from his pocket. 'If we can reach the top of the Tower we ought to keep these people at bay.'

They went up the narrow stairway

three steps at a time, the pursuers at their heels.

Presently a rush of cool air told them they had almost reached their objective.

Looking up, they saw the square opening that led out on to the flat roof of the Tower and, with a final spurt, reached it and scrambled through breathlessly.

'Quickly!' panted Lowe. 'Help me close the stone.'

With Jim's assistance he managed to raise the heavy square stone that covered the exit.

It fell into place just as the first of their pursuers reached the aperture and, catching him a heavy blow on the head, sent him crashing back into his companions.

'If we stand on the stone,' said Lowe, 'it'll take them some time to shift it.'

He drew in great gulps of the cool night air.

'We've got a moment's rest anyhow,' he continued. 'The question is, how can we make the best use of it?'

'We might escape from the Tower by climbing down the ivy — ' began Jim; but

Lowe shook his head.

'It wouldn't do any good if we did,' he said. 'They'll expect us to do that, and be waiting for us below. While we remain here we're comparatively safe.'

Ignoring the battering on the stone slab beneath his feet, he looked around him. The night was dark and clear, and the twinkling light of the Dungeness lighthouse appeared remarkably close.

Monotonously it flashed, went out, and flashed again. Jim, following the direction of his gaze, watched the light for a moment mechanically, and then suddenly he snatched Lowe's arm.

'What's the matter with the lighthouse?' he whispered.

'Matter with it? What do you mean?' asked the dramatist.

Jim looked at the watch on his wrist.

'There used to be ten seconds between each flash,' he said, 'and now there's nearly fifteen.'

'Perhaps they've changed the timing,' said Lowe absently.

'I thought they always kept these things the same,' muttered Jim; and then: 'Look, it's stopped altogether!'

The light had ceased its intermittent flashing and was now shining steadily.

'It must have been a breakdown,' muttered Lowe. 'Probably the mechanism has gone wrong.'

As the last words left his lips he drew in his breath with a sharp hiss.

'By Jove, I wonder!' he muttered.

'What?' asked Jim.

'If something's gone wrong with the lighthouse,' said Lowe, speaking rapidly, 'there'll probably be a look-out man on the gallery. If I could signal with my torch they might send help — '

'Try it!' broke in Jim excitedly.

Trevor Lowe drew his torch from his pocket, and at that moment the stone beneath them reared upwards under a sudden onslaught from the other side.

'We shall have to be quick,' said the dramatist. 'They've augmented their resources below and our combined weight won't be able to prevent them from getting through for long.'

He had learnt the Morse code during the war, and now he began to signal as quickly as his memory would allow:

'S O S. POLICE MESSAGE URGENT. S O S. REPLY IF YOU UNDERSTAND ME.'

He repeated the message again and again, watched eagerly the steadily burning light in the distance.

But the reply he hoped for did not come.

'The torch may not be powerful enough to carry the distance,' he said. 'Anyhow, we may as well keep trying.'

He began again, and this time he had scarcely repeated the message before a light flashed out faintly from below the brighter star point of the lighthouse's lamp.

As it winked unevenly Lowe read the message:

'S O S RECEIVED.'

Instantly he answered:

'GREYTOWER IN HANDS OF ARMED GANG. NOTIFY POLICE, HYTHE. HELP URGENT.'

The answering message came almost at once.

'WILL DO AS YOU ASK.'

'They're notifying Hythe,' said Lowe,

in answer to Jim's eager-question. 'If only — '

That was as far as he got, because the stone on which he and Jim were standing was forced violently upward and they were thrown off their balance.

They fell heavily to the roof of the Tower, and before they could recover and regain their feet the men who came pouring through the square aperture had thrown themselves upon them and rendered them helpless!

26

The Round-Up

Major Winning was feeling bored and not a little irritable. He had spent the evening at a public dinner in Hythe, which had developed into a succession of apparently endless speeches, and he had been thankful when the whole thing was over.

Driving along the High Street on his way back home, it occurred to him to call in at the police station and have a word with Superintendent Hartley.

'He's up at Mr. Winslow's place, sir,' said the desk-sergeant. 'You could get him on the telephone.'

'That's a good suggestion,' said the chief constable. 'Get the number, will you, Sergeant?'

The sergeant tried and failed. He looked up over the top of the telephone at the impatient chief constable.

'The Exchange say they can't get no

reply, sir, from the Exchange at Stonehurst,' and then before Winning could reply he went on speaking again into the mouthpiece of the telephone. 'You're sure o' that? What's wrong then? Oh, I see. All right.'

He put down the receiver and pushed the phone away from him.

'They say there must be something wrong with the line, sir,' he announced. 'They say they can't make 'em hear at all. They can't get no ringin' signal.'

Then the phone bell rang suddenly.

'Hullo?' he called, putting the receiver to his ear. 'Yes, this is Sergeant Butterworth speaking. Eh?' Winning saw his face change. 'What's that?' There was a long pause and then: ''Ere, 'old on a minute,' said the sergeant, and covering the mouthpiece with his hand, he looked excitedly across at Winning.

'They've just rung up 'ere from Dungeness lighthouse,' he said. 'They say they've just got a message flashed in Morse from the direction of Stonehurst, asking them to communicate with the police. They say the message said: 'Greytower in 'ands of armed gang; notify police, 'Ythe. 'Elp urgent.' They seem to think it may be a 'oax.'

Major Winning uttered a very major-like oath.

'Here, give me the telephone,' he said, crossing over to the desk and almost snatching the instrument from the sergeant's hand. 'Hullo!' he called. 'Is that the Dungeness lighthouse? This is the chief constable speaking. Repeat the message you received, will you?'

He listened while the voice at the other end of the wire repeated the message and explained the circumstances in which it had been picked up.

'Right,' said Winning. 'Thank you. You did quite right to notify us. No, I don't think it's a hoax at all.'

He banged down the telephone and turned to the listening sergeant.

'Get on to Ashford, Tenterden and New Romney,' he ordered, 'and call out all the reserves. Tell them the men are to be armed, and rushed to the four cross-roads just outside Stonehurst. I'll be there to meet them. I want every available man that can be spared.'

'You think this thing's serious, sir — ' began the sergeant.

'I do,' snapped Winning. 'I think it's very serious. Don't talk. Do what I tell you.'

The sergeant obeyed and the chief constable paced restlessly up and down, his brows almost meeting with the concentration of his frown.

It took the sergeant nearly fifteen minutes to get in touch with all the places that Winning had named. But at the end of the time he looked up with a sigh of relief.

'That's all right, sir,' he said. 'They'll be leaving almost immediately.'

'Good,' said Winning. 'Now, how many men can we muster?'

The sergeant scratched his head.

'Not more than half a dozen, sir,' he said doubtfully.

'Well, they're better than nothing,' said the chief constable. 'When you get hold of the men send them after me.'

The sergeant nodded, and Winning hurried out of the police station and got into his waiting car.

There was no traffic about, and he was able to keep up a good speed.

It was barely fifteen minutes after leaving the police station that he arrived at the cross-roads, and the place was silent and deserted.

Pulling up, he waited impatiently for the first contingent of the men he had ordered.

It came three minutes later: a big police car packed tightly with uniformed and plain clothes officials.

The inspector in charge came over to Winning and saluted.

'What's the trouble, sir?' he asked.

The chief constable briefly explained, and the inspector whistled.

'What do you want us to do, sir?' he asked.

'Wait here until the others arrive,' answered Winning, 'and then we'll go up to Greytower.'

The others arrived during the next ten minutes, and when Winning had collected the men in charge around him and explained the situation he sketched out his plan.

'What we want to do,' he said, 'is to take these men by surprise. They're armed, and we don't want any bloodshed if we can help it. My suggestion is that we leave the cars in the road and proceed up the drive leading to Greytower on foot. Are your men armed?'

'Most of them, sir,' was the reply.

'Right, then; we'll start,' said the chief constable. 'I'll lead the way.'

He got back into his car and turned it round in the direction of Stonehurst.

With the police cars following behind, he drove off, and presently reached the road into which the drive emerged.

At the beginning of it he stopped the car and got out.

'What do you suggest we do, sir?' asked the inspector from Ashford. 'Spread the men out and surround the place?'

'Yes,' said Winning.

The man turned away and began whispering instructions, and by ones and twos the crowd of policemen began to drift away into the darkness.

Major Winning followed cautiously up the dark drive and and stood twisting his moustache and staring at the house.

He was beginning to feel a little twinge of uneasiness.

Everything was very quiet, and there seemed no sign of any trouble at all. Had that message been a joke? If it had, it was going to be very awkward. He had taken the responsibility of calling out thirty policemen, and if there was no justification for —

A sharp whip-like report broke in on his thoughts. It was followed by a scream of pain and, turning in the direction of the sound, he saw one of the constables fall writhing to the ground, his hands clasping his leg.

As though the shot had been a signal, it was followed almost immediately by a staccato volley.

A bullet sang past Winning's ear so closely that he felt the wind of it and one of the inspectors dragged him down flat.

'They're firing from one of the upper windows, sir,' he whispered. 'Keep over in the cover of those bushes.'

'This is like Sydney Street,' gritted one of the inspectors, as the constable beside him went down, his hands clutching his stomach.

His companion sent a couple of shots in the direction of a pencil of flame that appeared momentarily in a lower window beside the front door.

A scream told him that his bullet had found a target and he gave a grunt of satisfaction.

'As long as their ammunition lasts,' he said. 'This looks like going on for a long time.'

'Wouldn't it be a good idea, sir,' said a plainclothes man, 'to try and rush the place? If we could once get under the shelter of the porch we should be pretty well protected while we broke down the door.'

'We'll try it, Jack,' said his superior. 'We'll take a dozen men and try it. Tell the others to keep on firing, so as to keep those fellows inside occupied.'

He moved away in the darkness and went round collecting his men.

'Now,' he said when they were all ready. 'When I say 'Right,' make a dash for the porch.'

He waited until a heavy burst of firing

broke out from the back, and then gave the signal.

In a concerted rush they made for the steps, stumbled up them and reached the comparative safety of the porch.

'So far, so good,' panted the inspector. 'Now we'll have the door down!'

He put the muzzle of his pistol to the lock and fired.

'Now, then,' he said. 'All together!'

The men with him hurled themselves at the stout door and it creaked under the onslaught of their combined weight. But it still held.

'Again!' ordered the inspector.

This time with a tremendous crash it flew open.

A hail of bullets greeted them from the darkness within, and three of the attacking party crumpled up and fell backwards down the steps.

'Blow your whistle for the others!' said the inspector. 'We've got 'em now!'

He hurled himself on a man who sprang at him out of the darkness, and they went down fighting desperately.

A police whistle sounded shrilly, and a

few seconds later the rest of the men came pouring in through the shattered door.

It was now a fight at close quarters. The crooks had no time to reload their weapons, and except for an odd shot here and there the firing had suddenly ceased.

'Well,' panted Major Winning a few minutes later speaking with difficulty through swollen lips and looking blearily through an eye that was rapidly becoming black, 'that was pretty hot while it lasted!'

He looked round at the sullen faces of the prisoners.

'Nasty looking bunch,' he remarked. 'Isn't that Japper over there?'

The landlord of the Crossed Hands, who was handcuffed to a burly constable, glowered at him, but said nothing.

'The inmates of the house are in the drawing-room, sir,' said an inspector, coming up at that moment. 'Trussed up like a lot of chickens. One of the men is releasing them now.'

The first to emerge into the hall was Trevor Lowe, and he greeted Winning with a smile.

'You and your men arrived just in time,' he said.

'Who sent that message to the light-house?' asked Winning.

'I did,' answered the dramatist. 'I managed to get away and reach the Tower. It was just after I'd sent the message they caught me again. Did you get the leader of this lot — a tall man with a mask?'

'Yes, sir,' said an inspector, 'but I'm afraid he's dead, sir. He's in the kitchen.'

'I'd like to see him,' said Lowe, and followed the man across the hall.

The masked man lay among the pile of petrol cans, but the mask had slipped from his face, revealing his heavy features rigid in death.

The front of his coat was soaked with blood, and he had apparently been shot in the general struggle.

Lowe was bending over him when he heard a muttered exclamation of surprise behind him, and looking round, he saw that Shadgold and Murley had come in and were standing staring in amazement at the dead man.

'What is it?' said Lowe quickly. 'Do you know this fellow?'

'Yes,' answered Shadgold. 'It's Locker!'

* * *

The rest of that night was a busy one.

From the smaller members of the gang, now thoroughly frightened and cowed, they succeeded in obtaining the names of the people who belonged to the organisation which Locker had brought into being.

From house to house they went, and by four o'clock in the morning had finished their task.

The only person who escaped them was Lady Thurley. When they went to take her they found that she was dead. She was lying peacefully in her bed, and the empty bottle of the drug which had killed her was still clasped in one nerveless hand.

It was a bedraggled group that came in the grey of dawn to the little police station at Hythe.

Mrs. Gordon-Watts without the heavy

make-up that she usually affected, looked a washed-out, rather pitiable creature, although her husband put on a certain rather false nonchalance.

Freeman, alias Netherton, was almost in a state of collapse, and his companion, Kenner, who had passed in Stonehurst under the name of Linney, was practically in the same condition.

Inspector Murley had recognised them both, in spite of their dyed hair and certain alterations which they had made in their appearance.

Only Toogood and Dr. Grendon appeared to be completely unmoved.

Lowe's first thought when the fight at Greytower had come to an end was for Arnold White, and he had been overjoyed when they had discovered his secretary, rather weak and ill but otherwise unharmed, in the cellar of Toogood's house.

Much against White's will, for he had wanted to hear all the news, Lowe had insisted upon packing him off at once to bed, under the care of Superintendent Hartley's aunt with strict injunctions that he was not to stir.

'And that's that,' remarked the dramatist when the prisoners had been charged and locked in cells. 'I must say I wasn't so very surprised when you identified the leader of this outfit as Locker.'

'Neither was I,' said Shadgold. 'I began to suspect who he might be when he started that long rigmarole about how clever he was, and how clever he was going to be. Locker could never help boasting. We used to pull his leg about it at the Yard.'

'That's why I guessed,' said the dramatist. 'I remembered what you told me, and when I saw the expression on your face I was pretty certain.'

'I wonder what put the idea into his head,' grunted Shadgold.

Lowe shrugged his shoulders.

'That we shall never know,' he replied. 'But, of course, the forming of this organisation was child's play to him. He knew most of the crooks who specialised in the various branches of crime, such as forgery, drug-running, burglary and blackmail. I've had a talk with Miss

Heyford, and apparently he called once on her aunt, Lady Thurley, who was being blackmailed. When he started this mass production of crime he remembered her and forced her by threats to come in with the rest. Her job was the blackmail end of the business. She moved in a good set and was very useful. By the way, they were extending their operations on the drug-side, so Freeman says. They were getting tired of paying the price for cocaine that they had to and were thinking of growing it themselves. As you know, it comes from a plant — the coca plant. Locker apparently conceived the idea of running up a factory in the middle of the village that was ostensibly to be used in the manufacturing of soap, but really would have concealed the huge greenhouses in which they were going to grow these plants. It would have been a profitable scheme if it had come off.'

'Who shot Calling?' asked Shadgold.

'Locker himself,' replied Lowe. 'I got the whole story out of 'Sniffy' Smith. Calling was kicking over the traces. He didn't mind burglary, that was his job.

But when he learned of the Scotland Yard men who were killed he kicked up rough. He told them he wasn't going to have anything more to do with them, and Locker, who was afraid he might squeal, decided to kill him. Calling got wind of this and came up to his friend, North, for protection. That was the night Jim Winslow first arrived in Stonehurst. But they got him in the grounds before he could reach North. Winslow and McWraith heard him scream. He managed to escape again, however, and rang me up from the village. He must have remembered meeting me and my interest in crime, and I suppose he rang me up because he was afraid to ring up the police, in case he might get himself into trouble. These fellows caught him again just as he came out of the call-box. They had a car with them, and they bundled Calling inside and took him to the Tower, where Locker shot him.'

'And I suppose,' said Murley in a low voice, 'that's where those other poor fellows were killed?'

Lowe nodded.

'Yes, it was a sort of execution chamber,' he replied. 'Their bodies were buried in the wood at the back of Greytower.'

'And the reason why they were killed,' said Shadgold, 'was because they had stumbled on to something.'

'They must have recognised Locker,' said Lowe. 'He had a house at Hythe. Only one member of the outfit knew who he was really, and that was Grendon. None of the others ever saw him without his mask.'

'Well, it's a pity we can't hang him,' said the inspector. 'But we've got enough evidence to hang his friends.'

He yawned.

'What a night!' he said, and Lowe smiled.

'I suppose that young lady will be all right, sir,' put in Superintendent Hartley. 'Miss Heyford, I mean. It was plucky of her to try and warn us after she had overheard her aunt and Mrs. Gordon-Watts discussing what was going to happen.'

'Very plucky,' agreed the dramatist. 'I

think she suspected something for a long time. You needn't worry about her, Hartley. Mr. Winslow's looking after her, and I should think it's quite likely he'll go on doing so.'

The superintendent raised his eyebrows.

'Like that, is it, sir?' he said, and his good-humoured face broke into a smile.

'Just like that,' replied Trevor Lowe. 'And now what about breakfast?'

* * *

The new landlord of the Crossed Hands pushed a foaming tankard across the beer-stained counter towards old John Tarley and the fat Mr. Criller paid for it.

'An' 'e said 'e bought the land?' he asked.

Old John poured a large quantity of beer down his wizened throat.

''E did,' he said, wiping his lips with the back of his hand. 'So there ain't goin' to be no more trouble about that. We shan't 'ave no factories spoilin' the view and ruinin' of the crops.'

'Just come back from their 'oneymoon, ain't they?' said Mr. Criller.

'Aye,' said old John. 'An' right well they look, too.'

'Where did Winslow get his money from?' asked a thickset farmer who was standing near by.

'That there Lunnon fellow got 'im a good job,' answered Tarley.

''E's 'avin' Greytower done up and the gardens all looked arter,' said Mr. Criller.

'Aye,' said old John Tarley, and signalled to the landlord by banging the bottom of his empty tankard on the counter. 'What you goin' to 'ave, Joe Criller?'

'Beer,' said Mr. Criller.

'Beer,' said the thickset farmer.

'Three beers,' said old John Tarley.

THE END

Other titles in the
Linford Mystery Library:

DENE OF THE SECRET SERVICE

Gerald Verner

Bound for Liverpool to board his Japanese ship, *Oki Maru*, a Korean seaman is murdered and his identity assumed by his killer. Then, after the ship sails, it disappears — presumed lost in a storm . . . The owner of a remote country house in Wales is pressured into selling it — then brutally murdered. Meanwhile, when secret documents relating to a draft treaty with Japan go missing from the Foreign Office, agent Dene of the Secret Service has orders to recover them . . .

LONELY ROAD MURDER

John Russell Fearn

Rosemary Lennox is horrified to find her best friend and neighbour, Mary Francis, strangled in her flat and it's not long before her husband, John Francis, is also murdered there too. The police question Rosemary, her friend and fellow lodger Bob McDonnell and their landlady Ellen Moreland, but they are unable to establish a motive. However, when Rosemary and Bob attempt to investigate, she discovers that all the evidence points to her friend . . .

THE HAUNTED GALLERY

John Russell Fearn

Baffling robberies and mysterious murders are the stock-in-trade of Miss Victoria Lincoln, private detective . . . After Professor Marchant dies, his house, Bartley Towers, is visited nightly by a sinister enemy, which frequents the gallery containing the Professor's collection of antiques and curios. When the detective investigates the case, she calls on the assistance of Caroline Gerrard . . . Thereafter, Miss Lincoln and Miss Gerrard investigate a series of bizarre cases, which are seemingly insoluble . . . until Victoria Lincoln gets to work . . .